JOKER
SONS OF HAVOC BOOK ONE

CLAIRE SHAW

CONTENTS

Chapter 1	1
Chapter 2	9
Chapter 3	23
Chapter 4	33
Chapter 5	40
Chapter 6	48
Chapter 7	63
Chapter 8	75
Chapter 9	97
Chapter 10	111
Chapter 11	130
Chapter 12	145
Chapter 13	163
Chapter 14	179
Chapter 15	195
Chapter 16	209
Chapter 17	227
Epilogue	244
Acknowledgments	249
About the Author	251
Social Media	253

Copyright This book is a work of fiction. The names, characters, places, and incidents are all products of the author's imagination and are not to be construed as real. Any resemblances to persons, organizations, events, or locales are entirely coincidental.

Joker. Copyright © 2022 by Claire Shaw. All rights reserved. No part of this book may be used or reproduced in any manner whatsoever without written permission from the author, except in the case of brief quotations used in articles or reviews.

For information, contact Claire Shaw.

Cover Design by Dee Garcia – Black Widow Design
Editing by Kim Lubbers – Knox Publishing
Formatting by E.C. Land – Knox Publishing
Proofreading by Alecia Rivers Goodman

❦ Created with Vellum

Can the broken really ever be free?

Joker

My best friend became the love of my life, and in the blink of an eye, she was gone. Ripped away from me with no warning. I'll never stop hunting for her.

She'll be mine.

Carrie

One minute I was in his arms, and the next, I was in hell. No one can save me, but me. I'm the Sons of Havoc Princess, and I'll rain down havoc to reclaim my life.

CHAPTER ONE

CARRIE

THE PAST

Bright lights, music, the smell of the shoe disinfectant, the sound of the balls on the lanes, and people laughing. I love the sounds of a bowling alley. My weekend and after school job was at the local bowling alley. The owner had taken a chance on me, and I was grateful. My folks weren't the greatest. Dad left before my little brother Johnny was born, and Mom was present, but not really. She was either drunk, high, or just not around.

Every day I would wish Mom would give up the drink and drugs. The feeling that your own mom would rather be drunk or get high than raise you broke a piece of me. Johnny was a sickly baby when he was born due to Mom still drinking and doing drugs while pregnant. I was all he had left; I was 12 years old when Johnny was born, and I loved him like my own. I took joy in caring for him and making sure he was clean and fed.

I could never understand why we were never enough for Mom. Why couldn't she love us like we loved her? Even after everything, she was still our mom, and we loved her.

The neighbor, Mrs. Clark, helped look after Johnny while I was at school and when I was at work. She was a lovely lady and helped all she could, but she was only just getting by herself and couldn't afford to help us as much as she wanted to.

We didn't want her money. The time spent in her warm, cozy, and inviting home, plus the meals she would cook for us, were more than enough. We felt safe and loved when we would go around to her house. She was the grandma we craved. It was truly when we felt our happiest, sitting around her kitchen table playing games or cozy on the sofa with a blanket watching movies.

Every so often, Mom would attempt to get clean and start trying to get herself together. She was always sorry and full of promises to be better. Sadly, they didn't last long, and as we grew older, it happened less and less until she just stopped trying at all.

Before Dad went away and Johnny was born, it was a happy home. I was always a daddy's girl. After Dad left, my mom had to step up and fill both roles. She struggled to find a job, and not long after Dad left, she found out she was pregnant. When Dad was around, they both always loved to party. Though once Mom was on her own, she started to spiral and party too hard until she couldn't stop.

I remember the day Dad left clearly. He gave me a hug, told me he loved me, and said I was his joy. He held me so tight and just kept saying he was sorry and how much he loved me. He told me I needed to be strong and look out for Mom.

I cried and begged him not to go. The sadness and despair on his face would never leave me. My dad was my whole world.

My dad was a member of the local MC, Sons of Havoc. Mom hated them. She used to say they were dirty animals and not to be trusted. The brothers I'd meet always seemed kind to me and were nice when I saw them. They looked scary, but they never made me feel scared. I always felt safe and precious. Their Princess, as they used to call me. When they came to the house, they would always take the time to say hi to me and give me hugs. A few of them once even had a tea party with me.

The only bright spot in my life other than Johnny was Jason. Jason was the boy next door and my best friend. We had lived next door to each other all our lives, and our dads were best friends.

Jason helped me with Johnny a lot and to buy food when I didn't have money to buy any, and Mom was on one of her benders, where she would disappear for days on end. Those days would scare me, being alone in the house with Jonny and no protection. Jason's dad was also a member of the Sons. Jason's mom had died when he was little, so it was just the two of them, and they were close.

His dad was away a lot on *'club business,'* which left Jason with no real adult supervision. So, Jason would take the gun his dad had in the house and stay with us. Together we were stronger.

Not long after my dad left, Mom started the hunt for a *'real man,'* as she put it, to replace Dad. My dad could never be replaced. The men she brought home were always as drunk or high as she was. I used to hide Johnny and me in my room, away from Mom and her men doing drugs and having sex in the living room.

The sounds coming from the living room, no child should ever hear. At first, they used to leave us alone, but as I started to grow and develop, the men used to stare and ask Mom if I was going to join them. I think that was the point Mom started to hate me. She would accuse me of flirting with them and trying to steal her men for myself. She was delusional. The men were all old, balding with beer bellies. She was just so desperate for love and attention.

One night, one of the men she brought home stumbled into my room and tried to get into bed with me. I screamed and tried to fight him off. It really scared Johnny, and he ran from the room. Luckily, Johnny ran next door to Jason's, and his dad Bull was home. Bull came and pulled the guy off me.

Jason held me while I sobbed, stroking his hand up and down my back, reassuring me I was okay, and he wouldn't let anything happen to me ever again. We could hear Bull shouting at my mom. He kept telling her how furious my dad would be to know his kids were living like this, not safe in their own home.

I begged Bull to tell me where my dad was. At that moment, I just wanted my dad, but he just shook his head and told me he couldn't with a sad smile and a hug. It was *'club business.'* He was sorry this happened, and if he could change it, he would.

On weekends when I would work at the bowling alley, Jason would spend time with Johnny. Sometimes they would come to meet me, and we would play in the arcade. Johnny loved the slot machines. I loved those times when we would play together and then have a few bowling games. Like a little family. I used to watch the other families around me and wish we could be like them. All nicely dressed and happy, smiling like we didn't have a care in the world, just spending time together.

I was jealous of them. I wanted what they had. Even at a young age, I knew my life wouldn't ever be like that. Maybe in my wildest dreams, one day, but I had to face reality. Johnny loved Jason and really looked up to him. He was a big brother who looked out for him, taught him to defend himself and how to be a man.

We were happy the three of us, with the adults making appearances every now and then. Bull was more of a parent than Mom and made sure there was food and money for whatever Jason needed. He even used to leave a little extra for us when he knew we needed it. You could see that he was proud of me, that I was doing what I had to do to take care of Johnny.

Things changed when we turned fifteen. I started to notice Jason was no longer the scrawny, short, spotty kid who was my best friend. His skin cleared up. He grew so tall and started to bulk up. He started to develop real muscles, and his voice started to change —get deeper and muskier. That was when my feelings changed. Whenever his finger would graze my arm, or he held my hand, butterflies would flutter in my stomach, and goose bumps would break out on my skin where his touch had just been. I would dream about him kissing me, those soft lips on mine. His behavior toward me never changed, except he now slept on the floor in the room Johnny and I shared instead of in the bed with me.

I missed his arms around me, the feel of his breath on my neck as he snuggled close behind me, keeping me safe. I was counting down the days till my sixteenth birthday. Not that sixteen was anything big, but it meant I was one year closer to being eighteen. That was the golden age when I could legally look after Johnny, and we didn't need to be worried about Child Protective Services coming and taking him away. Jason had promised me a surprise for my birthday. I couldn't wait to see what he had planned.

CHAPTER TWO

CARRIE

When my birthday finally came, Johnny went to stay with Mrs. Clark for the night. I had chosen a flowing floral dress in cream with a small pink flower pattern and my favorite pair of ankle boots. My blonde curls lay loose and free, flowing down my back. I had paired the dress with a necklace Dad had given me. It is a locket with a picture of Johnny, Dad, and me on one side and a picture of Jason on the other. Nerves rattle my body as I spritz on some perfume Mrs. Clark had bought me as a birthday present.

Jason turns up in a pair of dark jeans, a black t-shirt that clings to his more defined muscles, and black biker boots. He's starting to look more and more like his dad. He had told me that he planned to join the

Sons as soon as he was allowed. That worries me a little for his safety, but I know his dad and the other brothers would be there for him.

Just the sight of him standing at my door had my knees feeling weak.

"You look beautiful," he grizzles. His voice makes my stomach do somersaults.

"Thank you," I murmur nervously.

He takes my hand and leads me out to his truck. Sliding onto the seat, he closes my door and makes his way around the truck.

Jumping in, I ask him, "Where are we going?"

He looks over to me with his gorgeous brown eyes, winks, and says, "It's a surprise," laughing as he put the truck in drive and pulls away from the curb.

A short while later, he turns off the road and down this rough track between the trees, woods on either side. We drive until coming to a clearing that opens up with the most amazing view. We seem to be high up, and the view across to the sunset is breathtaking. Jason turns the truck around, so the bed of the truck is facing the view. Jumping out, I walk through the long grass to get a better look.

Not sure how long I had been standing there, I felt a pair of strong arms wrap around me and his breath near my ear.

"It's beautiful," I exclaim, not taking my eyes off the sunset.

"Not as beautiful as you," he whispers back.

We stand for a little while longer, just enjoying his arms around me and the view. "Ready for your surprise?" he asked.

"Oh my God, is this not the surprise?"

He chuckles and replies, "Too fucking cute, babe."

Grabbing my hand, he leads me back toward the truck. I notice for the first time that in the bed of the truck, he had laid a blanket out and some cushions against the cab. There's also a picnic basket. He helps me climb into the bed, and we get comfy against the cab.

He starts to empty the basket of all my favorite foods. I couldn't believe he had gone to so much effort and actually paid attention to what I liked. He smiles at me as he hands me a drink, and we tuck into the food.

Once we had finished eating, we laid back and relaxed. With my head on his chest and his arms around me, I truly think I am in heaven. He runs his fingers, trailing them up and down my arm, slowly and softly. His touch is so gentle.

Breaking the peace, he asks, "You want your present now?"

I look up at him, confused. "Is this not my present?"

He chuckled and pulled a black velvet jewelry box out of the picnic basket and handed it to me. My hands shook as I reached to take the box from him.

"Open it," he encouraged.

Shaking, I untied the white ribbon that was wrapped around the box and lifted the lid. Inside was a beautiful silver charm bracelet with 16 charms attached. I lifted it out of the box to get a better look. Inside the box were also two letter J charms, a heart charm, and a motorbike charm.

Taking the bracelet from my hands, he asked, "Do you like it?"

Looking him straight in the eye, I could see his panic.

"Oh, Jay, I love it," I croaked, my throat clogged with emotion. Besides the necklace from Dad, it's the most beautiful thing anyone has ever given me.

His face lit up with that amazing smile of his.

"I'm so glad you like it," he says as he adds the charms explaining each to me.

"The two Js are for Johnny and me. The heart is because you own my heart, and the bike means you can always ride free."

I can feel the tears threatening to drop. He's put so much thought into my present. He places the bracelet around my wrist and fastens it, his finger strokes up my arms, and he places a kiss on my hand.

"Did you mean it?" I asked tentatively. He looks at me, confused.

"Did I mean what?"

"That I own your heart?" I quietly confirm, almost too scared of the answer, could he really feel the same way as me.

His eyes never leave mine as he reaches out and wraps a hand around the back of my neck.

"Yes, I meant every word I said Carrie. I'm not sure when my feelings for you changed, but they have, and I want us to be together. Do you feel the same for me?"

I nod my head, too scared to say the words out loud in case this is all a dream.

His hand tightens on the back of my head, and his lips come closer and closer until finally, he kisses me. Slow at first, and then as I open up for him, the kiss grows hungrier and demanding. His tongue explores my mouth. His hands move to my lower back. Pulling away, we're both breathless. My hands wander and glide over his arms and down his stomach.

"Please, Jay, I want this," I beg.

"Carrie, are you sure? I'm not pressuring you. I'll wait till you're ready."

Nodding my head, I reach out to wrap my arms around his neck and kiss him. Not giving him the chance to stop me. He takes his hands from around my neck. They glide down my sides as he reaches the bottom of my dress, pulling it over my head leaving me in my bra and panties.

Feeling a little self-conscious of my plain white bra and so very unsexy underwear, I start to cover myself with my arms. His hands stop my arms.

"Please don't hide from me. You're the most beautiful girl I have ever seen."

Looking into his eyes, I can see his honesty. Removing my arms from across me, I grip the hem of his t-shirt and start to lift it over his head. It gets a little stuck, and he has to help me causing us to laugh. He began to remove his jeans and underwear until he's naked. I start to remove mine, but he stops me again.

"I want to unwrap you," he said seductively. Smiling, I lay back and let him remove my panties.

He's then leaning over me, unclipping my bra, so I'm laid naked in front of him. His eyes take every inch of me in. He licks his lips which makes me squirm and heat appears between my legs. He looks like he wants to eat me.

Bending down, he kisses me so hard and full of the passion of the situation, his hands stroking my arms and sides. His kisses move onto my chin, to my shoulder, and down to my breasts. Pebbling them with kisses, he takes my nipple into his mouth and sucks. A gasp escapes my mouth, causing him to stop and jump back.

"Oh, did I hurt you? Was it not good?" He looks so nervous and scared.

Giggling, I say, "No, it was nice, just didn't realize it would feel like that."

We both start to laugh. Neither of us knows what we're doing.

He starts to kiss me again, and his hands glide back down my sides getting closer and closer to my pelvis. Finally, after what feels like too long, his fingers run through my pubic hair, and he finds my clit. The sensation of his fingers on the little bundle of nerves causes me to gasp and my back to arch. Our breathing is becoming more erratic, and my whole body feels like it's on fire.

His fingers glide to my entrance, they stop just inside, and his eyes find mine. He's watching me intently as his fingers slide inside of me. His name slips from my lips as my back arches.

"Fuck your beautiful," he says. His voice is husky, and he's struggling to catch his breath.

Removing his fingers after pumping them into me a few times, he positions himself at my entrance, getting a serious look on his face.

"Beautiful, I'm sorry, but this is going to hurt. Fuck I wish it didn't, but it will be good after, I promise."

This is killing him. Running my fingers against his cheek and cupping his face, I tell him those three golden words, "I trust you."

His lips hit mine and devour me. I feel him push into me, and then he tears through my hymen, causing me to whimper at the sting. A tear slides down my cheek before I can stop it. Noticing, he kisses it away. He's holding himself so still. After a few beats, the pain eases.

"Please, Jason, make me feel good. I won't break, I promise."

With a slight smile on his face, he starts to move. Pressure begins to build inside, and every time he enters me, it causes me to gasp at the feeling. Soon his pace picks up, and the pressure's too much that I fall over the edge. It's a totally blissful feeling, screaming his name as I come.

Looking at him, he has a look of pure love on his face.

He starts to move again, his rhythm more erratic as he finds his release. With a roar, he comes cursing my name.

Holding each other tight the blanket wrapped around us, with Brantley Gilbert singing about being a "Grown Ass Man" in the background, looking up at the stars. I know this is heaven. I could lay here in this man's arms forever. Staying silent, both of us taking in what just happened, he speaks first.

"Thank you so much for trusting me with being your first."

Turning to face him, I cup his cheek.

"It was always you," I assure him, placing a soft kiss on his lips.

Lying back in his arms, we fall asleep wrapped around each other.

The next morning, the sun rising over the top of the trees is what makes me stir. Taking a moment to adjust my eyes and gather where I am, I'm lying in the back of Jason's truck, tucked safely in his arms.

Trying not to wake him, I slowly move out of his embrace, wrapping the blanket around my shoulders. I move to sit on the tailgate and watch the sunrise. It truly is a beautiful morning in more ways than one.

Taking a moment to process everything that had happened in the last several hours. I thought I would feel different. Maybe more grown-up, more like an adult. I'm sore, but otherwise, I don't feel different.

What I do feel different about is my feelings toward Jason. He made last night feel so special and made me feel so loved. It was the best birthday I ever had, and it will be one I'd never forget.

Feeling arms wrap around me, his voice all husky with sleep.

"Morning, beautiful."

Looking over my shoulder into his blue eyes, I whisper, "Morning," with a slight smile on my face.

"You, okay?" nervousness is noticeable in his voice. I love that he was as nervous as me.

"Perfect," I reassure him, stroking his forearms lightly with my fingertips.

We both sit in silence for a while, wrapped in each other's arms, just enjoying the peace and the sunrise, feeling content just to be with each other in silence.

With a sigh and a rumble of my stomach, I finally turn to face him.

"I need to go check on Johnny," I whisper, trying not to disturb the peacefulness of the clearing.

He nods his head in acknowledgment. Moving to climb out of the truck, Jason helps me down laughing as I nearly fall. Picking our clothes up, we hunt to find where they were thrown in our rush. Clipping my bra into place, I catch Jason watching. A blush creeps onto my cheeks as I remember his hands on the breasts I just covered up. I shyly look away. Picking up my dress, I slide in on. Once we're both dressed and standing a little awkwardly at the back of the truck, he wraps his arms around me.

"Come on, babydoll, we best get back," with a kiss to my head, we jump in the truck. Soon we're on our way back home.

Arriving home, Jason says he's got some errands to run for his dad, and he'd come see me tonight. Jumping out of the truck, I head for Mrs. Clark's to see Johnny. Rounding the house, I can see him kicking a soccer ball around the garden. That boy loves soccer. He supports a British team called Liverpool. Spotting me, he comes running over and hugs me.

"Hey, you have fun with Mrs. Clark?" Nodding, he tells me excitedly that they'd watched TV and she made pasta.

Mrs. Clark's pasta is the best. Mrs. Clark is standing in the doorway smiling.

"We had fun," she confirms.

"I have some fresh lemonade," she says as I make my way into the house.

We sit in her slightly outdated, but homely and welcoming kitchen, sipping on delicious lemonade while I catch her up on my birthday.

"He's a good one, that young man of yours," she observes smiling. "You can see from the way that boy looks at you, you're his love. He would do anything for Johnny and you. Even my old eyes can see that," she says, making me giggle.

"You're not old Mrs. Clark."

She really isn't that old, maybe late 60's, early 70's and fit as anything.

Her face turns serious. "Child, that boy is your future and your ride to a better life for both you and Johnny. Hold onto that." She now looks sad and as if she's deep in thought.

"You okay, Mrs. Clark?" I say as gently as possible as I don't want to upset her more. Turning to look at me with a small smile, she replies

"Yes, dear, just remembering my time with Mr. Clark, he's been gone many years now, but I still miss him."

My heart hurts for her. It must be devastating to love someone so much and lose them before your life together had really gotten started. Getting up from my chair, I go over and hug Mrs. Clark.

"Thank you for everything." She pats my arms and gives me a small smile. "Johnny, time to go," I shout, heading for the door.

Johnny comes running into the kitchen and hugs Mrs. Clark too.

"See you later," he shouts as he races out the door.

That boy does everything at speed. Laughing to myself, I make my way next door. Turning the corner into the front garden, I come to a halt. Johnny is standing with a man and two women who all look very business-like. Squaring my shoulders, I walk over to them and pull Johnny to me.

"Can I help you?" I ask, trying to sound older and braver than I feel.

A tingle shoots down my spine. Whatever these people want, I know it's not good.

CHAPTER THREE

JOKER

THE PRESENT

Today was a good day and exactly what I'd needed. My brothers and I had taken a ride out to see our Phoenix chapter. Help them celebrate the VP's wedding. When a brother gets married, it is always a reason for a party. Never could understand how a brother could stick with one woman. I had tried once, and it didn't end well. Staying free is the way to go for me.

The drive from Phoenix had taken us two days. I'm hot and sticky. Can't wait for a cold beer, a shower, and then find me some fun for the night. Don't get me wrong, my favorite place to be is on my bike. A nice long ride with the wind at your back is the most freeing sensation and always clears the fog and makes life clearer. It's my thinking space.

Pulling up to the clubhouse, we park our bikes in the very full lot. Bikes and cars are everywhere. Not only have we been celebrating Snake's wedding, but also one of our own being released from the big house after a very long stretch. Usually, we throw a big party and really help them settle back into life on the outside. Only this time, I am not looking forward to Reck being released.

Reck's daughter was my first love. She was my world, until one day, she and her brother just disappeared. Gone! We had tried everything to track them down. It seemed that Child Protective Services got wind that Reck was locked up and their ever-absent mother was not taking her role seriously. Both Carrie and Johnny were placed into the system.

Johnny was lucky and was adopted locally. We did manage to find him a few years ago, and he's now part of the club as a prospect. Sadly, we never did find Carrie, not that I stopped looking for her. We just hadn't broken the news to Reck.

Feeling a hand smacking me on the back brings me out of my memories. Turning, I face my best friend and brother, Tank.

"I can't wait for a shower and wet pussy," he says with his trademark grin.

The bastard is built like his name, but also goes through anything like a tank. Nothing stands in his way. Women flock to him, and he loves it. Biggest man-whore around!

We've been best friends since high school. He loved Carrie as much as I did. She was like his sister, and he'd treated her like she was precious to him. I know he misses her still. They had this weird non-sexual connection. If she ever needed to feel safe or loved and I wasn't around, Tank was her go-to. She was also the only one who could get through to him when his rage took over.

Laughing, I smack him back, and we head for the clubhouse. Pushing open the heavy door, smoke, the smell of weed, and loud rock music hit you in the face like a wall. These are the smells and sounds of home.

Making our way toward the bar at the back, Tank nods to the prospect for two beers. Grabbing my beer and nodding my thanks to the prospect, I turn to rest against the bar and take in the room. Brothers with old ladies are relaxing, and the sweet butts are huddled in a corner waiting for the old ladies and girlfriends to leave so the party could really start.

I sit at the bar for a while, shooting the shit with my brothers and catching up. The long day starting to catch up with me, I make my way out to my bike to grab my stuff from my saddlebags. While making my way across the parking lot, I can make out a shadow across the road. Slowing my walk a little, I try to get a better look.

Not being able to see much, I make my way to the gatehouse. Thinking if I could get closer to the shadow, I'd be able to make out who it might be. They are hiding a little, but something makes the hairs on the back of my neck stand up. Getting closer, I can make out the shadow a little better, it seems to be a woman, and she is staring at the clubhouse.

"Can I help?" I ask, trying to keep my voice friendly so as not to scare her. She is an older woman, eyes large with fright.

"Noo . . ." she stutters, turning and running back into the shadows toward a car.

She jumps in and speeds away before I can make a move.

"Alright, man?" a booming voice said behind me with a large hand landing on my shoulder.

I turn to Wolf standing behind me, eyeing the spot the woman was just standing.

"Yeah, brother, not sure what she wanted. I asked, but she ran."

He looked me over, something in his eyes telling me he had also felt that something was wrong. Wolf is a founding member, but also a bit of a psychic. He would get these vibes or feelings when shit is going to go down. But this time, I'd felt it too, and he knew it.

"Take it easy, son. I agree, somethings coming," he growls, turning and making his way back to the party.

I couldn't agree more with that statement. It's like I could feel it in my bones. Something is coming whether we want it to or not. I make my way into the gatehouse to make sure the prospect on duty is paying attention.

After speaking with the prospect, I make my way back to my room. Lying on my bed, I still can't shake the feeling. Something is brewing. I know the woman from tonight is the key to all this. After tossing and turning for a few hours, I finally find sleep.

The next morning, I make my way into the kitchen in search of coffee. A few of the brothers are finishing breakfast before we head into church. Today is the day Reck gets out of the big house. I'm happy to see him as he had played a massive part in our lives growing up, but also dreading it at the same time. I'm not sure how much he knows. Does he know he has a son? Does he know about Carrie? He loved Carrie with everything, and she was always a daddy's girl. She used to look at him like he'd hung the moon. The same way Tink, our Princess, looked at BJ, our Prez. Another daddy's girl.

Taking my coffee with me into church, I take my place around the table. BJ, our Prez, is at the head of the table with my old man, Bull, to his right as VP. Once we have all settled down in our places, Prez bangs the gavel.

"Well, brothers, let's start the good news, our man Reck is to be a free man today."

The room erupts into cheers and fists banging on the table. BJ lets the boys have this moment before bringing them to order again.

"Now, yes, it's a good thing he's free, but there is going to be a life adjustment to being on the outside. We need to make sure we do all we can to help him find his feet again."

Meeting my eyes, he knows my question.

"Joker, I know what you're going to say, and no, he doesn't know Carrie is missing, and he doesn't know he has a son. Once he's back at the clubhouse, I'll have a sit down with him and break the news."

Raising his hand as I open my mouth, he carries on.

"It was his choice, Joker, he requested he know nothing of the outside. Only way he could cope being on the inside."

Knowing my Prez is right, it would have only made his time on the inside worse, knowing he was helpless to protect those he loved. It had killed me not being able to protect her and Johnny.

We finish the rest of church, going over how the businesses are doing and a charity run we have coming up. Prez asks Bull and me to stay behind.

Once the brothers leave and the doors close, Prez levels me with a stare.

"Son, I know you feel we aren't doing enough to find Carrie, but trust me, I'm doing everything I can to find her. She's our Princess and means something to every brother here," he says. I nod my head as I feel my throat closing with emotion.

Getting up and leaving them to it, I make my way through the bar and out to my bike. I need to clear my head a little before I see Reck again. Getting on my bike, my baby girl, on the tank is a portrait of Carrie. I make my way out of town and along the back roads, feeling the wind and the road beneath me lets me clear my head and sort my feelings out. Making it only a short ride as I know we would be leaving soon to collect Reck, I make my way back to the clubhouse.

Driving through the gates, I can see the brothers are all getting ready to move. Falling into formation behind my pops and next to Tank, Prez gives me a nod.

Heading out together as one with the prospect behind in the truck with Reck's bike on the back, we make our way to the prison.

After about an hour, we pull up in front of the prison. Dismounting my bike, I make my way over to the truck to help unload Reck's bike and also check on Johnny. Johnny is a prospect, but also Reck's son. Only Reck doesn't know he's his son.

Slapping Johnny on the back, I ask, "You okay, bro? You ready for today?"

He turns to look at me, but I can't get a read on his face. Bro's got an excellent poker face. I can never tell how he's feeling.

"As good as I can be, considering I'm about to meet the man who doesn't know I'm his son," he grunts out with a shrug of his shoulders.

"I know, man, and I'm sorry it's not in better circumstances that you're meeting him. But we will make it right, I promise."

The noise of the gates opening distracts us as the boys closest to the entrance start to shout and holla. Clearly, they've released Reck. Giving Johnny's shoulder one last squeeze, I head over to join my Prez and my old man.

Walking through the gates is a man who is thankful to be on the other side, but also looks a hell of a lot older than he should. The boys all cheer as Prez and

Bull greet him with man hugs and back slaps. By the time Reck is standing in front of me, we just stare at each other, not saying a word. After a few beats, a grin appears on his face.

"Well fuck me, Jason, you've really grown into a man," he states while grabbing hold of me and hugging me.

Pulling away from me, he looks at my cut. "Always knew you were club. It's in your blood."

"Wouldn't have it any other way," Bull chimes in.

Smirking back, I reply, "Good to see you, Reck."

"Let's get this back to the clubhouse," Prez shouts.

We all mount up, and Reck mounts his bike while stroking the tank, his hands slowly starting her up. He closes his eyes and revs her a little. A total look of peace forms on his face. I can see Prez and Bull smirking like they know how he feels. Once Reck has had his moment with his bike, Prez gives the signal, and we all ride out.

CHAPTER FOUR

JOKER

Reck has been home a few days now; he seems to be settling in okay. The boys had been partying pretty hard. We were all sitting in the lounge room when Reck comes in.

"Off to see my girls," he chuckles as he's heading for the door.

My eyes instantly find Prez.

"Reck, I want a word before you go," Prez demands as he gets up and heads for church.

"Bull, Joker, join us," he finishes.

Taking a deep breath, I get up and follow them down the corridor to church. Once in the room, I close the door as I'm last in.

I choose to stay standing near the door. Reck is looking from Prez to Bull and back again.

"What's going on?"

He asks with a slight hardness to his voice, like he knows something is up.

Prez starts, "Brother, I know you requested to know nothing about what happened on the outside while you were inside. We respected that wish. Your ol' lady didn't handle you being sent down well and spiraled."

Reck's face grows hard. Wiping his hand down his face, he says, "Fuck, I knew she wouldn't. She hated this life and was a useless ol' lady."

I grunt in agreement, but otherwise keep quiet.

"Not long after you went inside, she found out she was expecting again. You have a son, Reck." Prez continues, "Your son is the prospect, Johnny."

The shock on Reck's face fades to the biggest, genuine smile a guy could have

"I have a son, and he's club?" Reck asks.

Prez nods, letting him have this moment before they break the bad news.

"There's more, brother. Your ol' lady couldn't cope. Turned to drink and drugs. Carrie did what she could, but fuck she was a stubborn, strong girl and hid a lot of what was happening."

Taking a breath, Prez breaks it down, "Child Protective Services got involved and took the kids. We found Johnny and looked after him. But fuck, brother, I'm sorry we haven't found Carrie yet. We're looking, and we won't stop," Prez promises.

Reck had gone white and is shaking with so much rage. His hands fist on the table, and he's visibly shaking.

Rising from his chair, fists still on the table, he grinds out.

"What the fuck do you mean you don't know where my girl is?"

Prez never wavers, looking Reck straight in the eye, "CPS took them before we could step in, and they were sent to separate foster homes. Johnny stayed local, but Carrie didn't. We have been searching for her ever since they took her. We have every resource on this, and we will find her," Prez promises.

Reck takes a deep breath and turns to me. Clearing my throat, I confirm, "I'll find our girl, and I'll bring her home." Hoping the conviction I feel comes across in my voice.

After a moment, he nods his head and comes to me. Wrapping his hand around the back of my neck and leaning close, he growls.

"I want in, and our girl is coming home. Can see you love her son, going to need that story soon."

Moving out of his way, he leaves church heading for his bike. I move to follow, but Prez stops me.

"Leave him, son. Give him the wind to sort his head out. Heavy news we just laid on him."

Lowering my head, I leave church and head to find Johnny. Best to warn him Reck knows he's his son. Finding Johnny in the garage, working on his bike, I ask him to join me outside. Taking a seat on the top of the picnic table, he sits next to me.

"Prez just told Reck about Carrie and also that you're his son," I warn.

Johnny looks down and says, "That why he took off like his ass was on fire a few moments ago?"

I put my hand on his shoulder as reassurance.

"Nothing to do with you, Johnny. Fuck, you should have seen the smile on his face when he found out you're his son. His leaving had everything to do with Carrie," I assure him. "Back in the day, your sister was a daddy's girl, and your dad worshipped her. It's a man's job to protect his family, and Reck is going to feel like he failed." I give him a moment for it to sink in. "He's going to need us to make sure he knows he hasn't failed. He was inside protecting his brothers, his other family. A hard spot to be put in."

As Johnny is still a prospect, I can't share too much club business with him, but it is his dad and sister, so I give him what I can. Making my way across the lot back to the clubhouse, I need to speak with Wire. Wire is our resident computer genius. If he doesn't know it, then it's not worth knowing. Catching up to him, I fling my arm around his shoulders.

"Any luck finding my girl?" I ask, praying he has something.

"Sorry, Joker, I'll keep looking, but her files from our CPS will have been transferred to the new area, but not knowing when or where makes it harder to look for," he says, sounding as deflated as I feel. "I recently heard of a new hacker on the scene with mad skills. Had a few run-ins with him. Might reach out and see if he can help. Worth an ask."

Now, this sounds more hopeful. Smacking him on the back, I tell him, "Fuck yeah, anything is worth a shot."

Heading for the bar, I grab a beer. Feeling a hand on my arm, I know it's a club girl.

"Hey, baby," she purrs in my ear.

Turning, I see Nikki standing next to me, wearing hardly any clothes, so her fake as fuck tits are nearly falling out her top.

"Nikki," I say, trying to sound as bored as possible, hoping she gets the hint.

"Fancy some fun, big boy?" she giggles.

Do women really think this shit is a turn-on? Removing her hand from my shoulder, I tell her, "Not tonight, Nikki. Go please another brother."

Stepping away from her, I make my way over to the table Tank, Bull, and a few other brothers are sitting at shooting the shit.

Sitting down, Bull turns to me.

"Seems Reck took it better than I thought he would."

Bull is named as he is, because he is as moody as a Bull and can smell bullshit from a mile off.

"Yeah, still kills me," I grunt.

Bull just nods his head

"She means a lot to all of us, son. She's family, our Princess. Here is where she belongs, and we will get her back."

I really hope he's right.

Halfway through the night, we end up outside with a bonfire. Reck had returned and seems a little calmer. He's currently sitting around the bonfire with a girl on his knee and his head between her tits. Our club girls are the best around, not whores, but just fun girls who need a home, a place to belong like all of us, and happen to like sex. The only bad one out of the bunch is Nikki. She's never really fit in with the others, and you can tell the other girls don't like her. They steer clear of her drama.

Feeling like I'm done for the night, I start to head back to the clubhouse. As I pass Reck, he grabs my arm, slurring his words a little. He tries to say, "You find my girl, promise me."

Patting him on the back, I reply, "I promise."

With that, he goes back to the girl on his knee. I head to bed and dream of having Carrie in my arms again.

CHAPTER FIVE

CARRIE

Feeling a little hand on my arm brings me out of my sleep. I try to move my head, but the pain is too much and I groan.

"Keep still, Mom, it's okay," Beau reassures me.

God. It's bad this time. I take a moment to take stock of my injuries. My whole body feels bruised, but nothing is broken. I attempt to get up slowly and make my way into the bathroom. The walk from the bed to the bathroom is pure agony. Holding onto the sink for support, I slowly raise my head to look in the mirror.

What greets me makes me suck a breath in. It looks like someone had tried to murder me. But then again, that's not too far from the truth. My left eye is swollen shut, and my right cheek is bruised, my lip is split, and there's dried blood on my lower lip. Lifting my tank top, I can see I have bruising on my ribs. Marks were left on my arms and breasts where he'd grabbed me. I honestly do not want to check the rest of me.

Slowly using the toilet, it is not a surprise when it's painful. He clearly had got a few good shots to my kidneys which would explain why my back hurts. Stripping out of my tank top and shorts, I reach in and switch the shower on. Once it's at temperature, I slowly step in and let the water wash it all away. Curling up in a ball, I let my tears fall. I would never cry in front of him.

He would see it as weakness and feed off of it. Well, fuck him. I'm not weak. Crying is not weak. I'm the motherfucking Sons of Havoc Princess, and I'll claim myself back. I was raised by badass men who know how to treat a woman. I'll bide my time, and once I'm able to get Beau and me clear, I will.

Pulling myself together, I clean up and get out. I don't like leaving Beau alone for too long. Drying and dressing in a clean tank and a comfy pair of jeans, I head back into the bedroom. Otherwise known as our prison. He only lets us out when he wants to, for his own pleasure.

Snuggling down on the bed, I hold my son close to me. I must have dozed off as I'm awoken by Agnes bringing us food. Agnes is an angel and also a prisoner here, but she's been here so long that she's allowed a little more freedom than me. Sitting up, I accept the tray from her, which has two bowls of soup and some crackers plus some fruit. I give her a weak smile as I can see the concern etched into her face. She's so kind-hearted and deserves so much better than this life. How she had ended up here is her story to tell.

Getting Beau to sit up, we both eat our soup in quiet. He doesn't like noise, so we keep as quiet as possible at all times. How I wish Beau could be a normal little boy. He would love to run in the grass, play ball, and just run free like any 10-year-old should. He doesn't allow him to go to school, so I homeschool him as much as I can with books Agnes gets for me. He's such an intelligent boy.

He knows who his dad is and how much we love each other. His dad, Jason, is my world and my true love. I often think about what he's doing now. Is he thinking of me, or has he moved on? I have one photo of Jason and me when we were teens. It's like looking at another lifetime. But I'm determined to make my way back, even if it's just for Beau's sake, as he should know who his dad is.

We hear the front door slam shut, and Agnes jumps.

"Shhh, it's okay. I'll take this and keep him appeased so you can rest," she whispers.

Kissing the top of my head and kissing Beau's, she shuffles out of the room with the tray and pots. I listen to her make her way back downstairs. God, I hope he's had his fill today and leaves us all alone for the rest of the night.

I strain to hear her downstairs to check what mood he is in. All seems to be quiet, so I relax, but not fully. In this house, you can never fully relax and let your guard down. Holding Beau closer to me, we both drift off to sleep.

Waking the next morning, I feel slightly better. Popping some Advil, I get ready for the day. Letting Beau sleep a little longer as his little body needs it. Watching him sleep from the doorway, I can't believe my boy would be 10 soon.

It kills me that he's not going to have a birthday party to celebrate—no cake, no games, no presents, and no friends around. He should be enjoying his childhood and having experiences most children take for granted. Stroking his hair, I make a promise that I'm going to get us out of this.

Slowly waking him, "Morning buddy, time to get up," I say softly while stroking his head.

"Five more minutes," he grumbles while rolling over and hiding his head under the covers. This makes me chuckle as Jason was always the same with getting up.

"Come on, Beau, you know it's time to get up. I've already let you sleep ten minutes longer."

With a groan, he flips the covers back, and body rolls out of the bed dramatically, making me laugh. Just as I'm laughing, a banging starts on the door, and his nasty voice shouts.

"Clearly, you two have done all your chores if you have time to be laughing. Get your lazy fucking asses up and get shit moving."

His outburst causes us to jump into action. Rushing to finish getting ready, we make our way downstairs. Heading straight for the kitchen, I start his breakfast while Beau heads for the living room to clear up his mess from last night. I'm sure the room is covered in empty beer bottles as usual.

Once his breakfast is on the table, he comes in and sits down. After a few mouthfuls, he declares, "This is shit. Call this food? Why can't you do anything right!"

Gripping the edge of the plate, he flings it in my direction, and I just manage to duck as the plate catches my forehead. He's up like a shot, grabbing me by my hair and dragging me out of the kitchen toward the basement. I try to stop him by grabbing onto whatever I can, but he just laughs. Still dragging me by my hair, he walks into the basement, locking the door behind him.

Flinging me onto the metal bed in the middle of the room, he goes to the restraints attached to the headboard. He forces my wrists into the restraints and then my ankles, leaving me spread out on the bed. His eyes rake over me, making my skin crawl and my stomach revolt.

Licking his lips, he says, "You will learn your place bitch. You dirty little whore."

Taking the pocketknife out, he cuts my clothes away from my body. I refuse to turn my head and keep my eyes fixed on the ceiling. I will not show him weakness. Hearing the denim of my jeans ripping, I try to go to my happy place. He removes the jeans, and I feel air on my skin. He makes his way to my tank top and removes that also, leaving me lying there in my bra and panties.

I can see the evil in his eyes and his heavy breathing as he's getting off on seeing me lying there, at his mercy. With a chuckle, he trails his finger slowly down my face and neck, between my breasts and down my stomach. As he starts to reach the edge of my panties, I can hear his breathing change to small pants as it excites him more. Still refusing to close my eyes, I focus on the ceiling and try to think of happy thoughts.

"You will know who owns you, pet," his fingers continue down the edge of my panties and across my thighs. "Maybe you need to learn who is in control."

He steps away from me and makes his way to the chest of drawers that sits against the wall. He removes a few objects from the drawers and makes his way back over to me. He places a blindfold over my eyes and secures it behind my head. Darkness engulfs me. I start to panic a little at not being able to see where he is. I flinch as I feel him near my ear; he places earplugs into my ears. The panic is getting worse, and my breathing is becoming erratic. Being unable to see or hear anything, I can't tell what he's going to do next.

I lie there waiting for his next move. But nothing! I wait and wait, but nothing. I'm not sure how long I had been lying there. I know I need the toilet. Couple that with not being able to see or hear is torture. He's showing me I need him, and he can make me do anything he wants. However, the only point he had proven is that I need to find my inner badass and show him whose daughter I am.

After what feels like an eternity, I suddenly felt a hand on my chin, gripping hard. The blindfold is removed, and I blink to adjust to the light now shining. He is grinning down at me with his evil malicious smile. He removes my earplugs while not being gentle at all.

"How is my little pet now?" He runs his hands along my sides. "I'll break you, and I'll enjoy watching you shatter," the look in his eyes scares me down to my bones.

He truly is pure evil.

CHAPTER SIX

JOKER

Reck has taken the hunt for Carrie seriously. He's tried contacting Child Protective Services to see if they would be willing to give him any information on where she was fostered. Fuckers were not helpful and couldn't care less that a man misses his daughter.

Wire is doing all he can. He'd contacted this new hacker whizz guy called Webbie, what a dumbass name. Wire had explained the situation, hoping this guy has a heart and will agree to help us.

I make my way to Wire's room to check on how he's doing. Knocking on the door, he shouts to come in.

"Brother, it could've been anyone at the door." He points to a screen off to the side of the full wall of computer screens he's staring at. I can see a camera pointed at the door. Clever fucker! Taking a closer look at the screens, I can see a few are different views from around the clubhouse and surrounding area, like the access road and a few of the woods around us. A few of the screens are feeds from around town—the road in and road out, Main Street, and then club businesses. Each screen is labeled with what it's showing. Brother is smart and I'm glad he's head of our security. Seems he thinks of everything, including the screens that show our officers' houses, mainly the outside, as we still respect their privacy.

I roll my eyes. "Any news?"

He keeps typing at his keyboard, fingers flying quickly over the keys.

"Webbie agreed to help in return for a marker."

Rubbing my hands over my face, I let out a breath.

"Need to take that to church, brother."

"Already called Prez, and he's calling church shortly."

Clearly, Wire is a few steps ahead of me.

"Great. Hopefully, brothers will agree to this Webbie's marker."

He grunts in agreement, not taking his eyes off the screens.

"Can't see it being a problem. It's for Carrie."

Hoping he's right, I leave him to whatever he's working on. Knocking on Prez's door, he tells me to enter. Looking up from his desk, he says, "Wondered how long it would take."

Sitting down on the sofa, I rest my head in my hands. "This is all getting to me. I just want my girl back."

Prez gives me a moment before he speaks. "I know, son, I would feel the same as you if anything happened to Pip. The woman is my life. But trust in your brothers and trust in your club to do everything they can to get your girl back. Remember, she's not only your girl, but Reck's daughter and our Princess. We look after our own. We're family."

I know my Prez is right. Brothers would die for each other and their families.

"Thanks, Prez, I needed to hear that," he gives me a sympathetic look.

"Just as long as you know it. Sometimes we still need to hear it confirmed."

Taking a deep breath, I get up.

"Church in an hour," are Prez's last words as I leave his office. A short ride is just what I need.

Pulling back into the clubhouse an hour later, Johnny tells me nearly everyone is in church already. I pick up the pace and slip into church. Wire comes in not long after, and Prez bangs the gavel.

"Brothers, this is not a normal church. We're here to discuss our efforts to find Carrie."

A few murmurs go around, and Reck bangs his fist on the table.

"About fucking time," he bellows.

Prez bangs the gavel again to get everyone's attention.

"Wire here has been doing some digging, and some hacker extraordinaire has agreed to help us. But he wants a marker from the Sons in return."

I sit upright in my chair, and Reck also sits straighter, both of us eyeing the brothers, daring them to say no.

"A marker is a serious commitment and needs to be put to a vote. Need you all to really think about this clearly. Sons are men of their word. We give this marker we agree to one deed, no questions asked."

I know Prez has to cover all his bases, but I'm pissed by his speech. By the look on Reck and Tank's faces, so are they.

"Right, let's vote," he says to end our thoughts.

I can feel the nerves racing through me as the vote goes around the table. I know Prez said to trust in my brothers, but that still doesn't help. As the vote goes around the room, everyone seems to be voting yes. The vote gets to Wolf, and he takes a few moments, and his gaze flits from me to Reck. After what feels like a lifetime, he votes yes. It continues around the room until it reaches Bull and Prez. Bull votes yes, giving me a wink. Prez brings down the gavel.

"Vote is a yes. We owe this Webbie a marker. Make it clear though Wire, nothing illegal. I won't put the club at risk."

Wire nods his head and leaves the room. Reck turns to me, and I can see the relief across his face.

A few days later, we're all sitting around the bar when Wire comes rushing into the room with a load of papers in his hand.

"Webbie came through!" he shouts, causing me to leap from my chair and rush to meet him.

"CHURCH NOW!" Prez bellows, and everyone moves.

I'm first in my seat while everyone else gets in. Prez is huddled in the corner with Wire. I know he would want to brief Prez first before the rest of us. Prez hates doing anything blindly. Getting the table to order, Prez starts.

"Wire's hacker friend has come through and managed to get hold of the foster file. Boys, you're not going to like it. Seems after being in a few foster homes, Carrie was released back into the care of Julie."

This news causes Reck to lose his shit.

"Calm down, Reck, there's more!" Prez says in a menacing manner. "Seems they allowed this, as Julie married some guy who seemed stable a few counties over, and they wanted to be a family. Wire is getting everything he can on where they may be now and what's happened since then. We're getting closer."

The atmosphere in the room is a mix of rage and disgust that any Child Protective Service would release a child to some druggie. Being with Mom is not always best.

The wait to see what Wire and Webbie find feels like the longest of my life. We spend days just sitting around doing nothing. I try to find things to keep me occupied and work in the garage we have at the clubhouse cleaning and servicing my bike. Tank and I spend some time in the gym and in the ring sharpening my skills. I also hang out with Reck and Bull at the range the club owns. It feels good to let off some steam and reconnect with Reck.

Finally, they have a few addresses. The addresses are a few towns over. As if she could have been this close all this time. That thought makes my rage increase. Prez starts to team us all up and then hands each team an address. In my team, it's me, Tank, Reck, and Wolf. The other two teams are led by Prez and Bull. With our instructions given, we head to our rooms to gear up. I make sure I'm dressed in black and packing my trusty Glock. Just as I'm heading for the door, I think twice and step back to grab my knife. You never can be too careful.

Making my way out to my bike, I can see the boys are ready. Reaching my bike, I look over at Tank. He looks straight at me and gives me a chin lift. He knows how much this means to me. I need my girl back. Prez makes his way outside and to his bike. He raises his hand, and everyone quiets down to listen.

"We know in this life nothing is forever, but be careful tonight brothers and come back safe."

With his speech over, he makes a fist, and all bikes start up.

The noise of all the bikes together is deafening, but also an amazing sound that settles my soul. Prez then extends his finger and makes a circle with it, which means we're off. Each team makes their way to the address they were given.

The ride takes around forty-five minutes, and we pull over a few miles out so we don't introduce ourselves too early. We want the element of surprise. Pulling off the road, we hide our bikes behind some bushes on the edge of some woods.

"The address is just through these trees," Tank says while consulting the GPRS he has. Each team has one, which allows us all to track our position and also each other.

Tank takes the lead, and we follow him through the woods, trying to be as careful as we can. We don't know what's in these woods. We walk for a few miles and then come to the edge of a property line. Getting into position, we scope out the area. Wolf climbs a nearby tree with his rifle on his back. He gets into a good position and uses the scope to view the property. Wolf is a fully trained sniper, the best.

Sitting in the dark, waiting for Wolf to do his thing, is nerve-racking. My adrenaline is pumping. Wolf's deep voice comes through the comms.

"All clear looks deserted. Move in!"

With that, we slowly make our way toward the buildings. Coming around the back of what looks like a barn, I peer in the window. The place is dark, but I can make out an old car and some farm machinery. Moving around to a door, I test the handle and find it open. Using my flashlight, I make my way inside.

Looking around, it does all seem to be farm machinery—all rusted and outdated. The place gives me the creeps, and something feels off about this place. I keep looking, and toward the back, an area has been cleared. Plastic sheeting covers the walls and floor. A metal table is off to the side, with a bunch of bloody tools scattered across it. In the middle is a metal chair with restraints attached. The hairs on the back of my neck are now standing at attention. What the fuck is this place?

Reaching for my comms, I say, "Brothers, is the house clear?"

A grainy voice replies, "Clear. Someone's been here, but not for a while. No girly shit anywhere."

I feel myself relax a little, at least that's something.

"Brothers, you need to see the shit in the barn. Fuck, it's like a torture chamber or some shit. Wolf, man, you need to see this."

"On my way," is the reply.

Taking a closer look, I can see what looks like a hospital metal gurney with restraints attached pushed up against a wall. Blood stains the top. In the far corner is a large sink with a whole load of chemicals and large metal barrels.

"Holy fucking shit," is the brothers' reactions to seeing the back of the barn. Wolf is looking over everything.

"Professional," is his take on it, and it's the same as mine.

"Whoever's place this is, knows what they are doing."

"What's in the barrels," Tank says as he makes his way over to them.

"Don't touch!" Wolf barks at him.

"Jesus, sorry, brother," Tank says, looking at Wolf with a wary face.

"The chemicals under the sink are for decomposing bodies. Them barrels will have bodies and acid in them," Wolf replies.

This fact makes our faces pale, and we all step away from the barrels. Who the fuck is using this place? I switch my comms to one where Prez and Bull can hear me.

"Prez got an issue. Seems our address is being used by some murdering weirdo. Torture chamber and barrels with bodies in acid. Freaky shit."

"Jesus fuck!" is the only reply I get from Bull.

"Take pictures and get back safe," Prez instructs.

Nodding to Reck, I let him know Prez's order, he starts to take pictures. Tank goes to keep watch, and Wolf is still examining the tools.

"Brother, what is this shit?"

Wolf looks me straight in the eye. "Not good."

This is exactly what I didn't want to hear. Had this freak got Carrie and been doing this shit to her? Is she already dead? Hurt somewhere? This had only left me with too many questions. I can see the pain in Reck's face. He's thinking the same as me. Not wanting to get too stuck in my own head, I make my way outside.

Taking a moment to myself, I think back to the last time I'd held my girl in my arms. It was her birthday, and she had just given me the best present ever.

I can't believe it. The most beautiful girl I had ever seen is lying in my arms, and we just shared the most amazing moment together. I truly feel like the biggest, richest man in the world, that Carrie trusted me enough to be her first, and it means the world to me that she's mine. I know we're both underage and deemed not mature enough to make the decision, but all the crap we'd gone through makes us mature enough.

It all just feels right. Like this is supposed to be how it is. Carrie makes me feel things I don't realize I could. I want to wrap her up and keep her safe. She has the purest heart of anyone I know. No matter what life throws at her, she still chooses to smile and see the good in the situation. She amazes me every day with how strong she is. My girl is a badass through and through.

Stroking my fingers along her arm, I hold her tighter to me as if she can disappear into dust at any time. Just the feeling of her next to me, head lying on my chest while she sleeps, it shocks me how I can feel this way for another person.

Losing my mom young was hard. Dad does what he can, but he's not great with his feelings. Mom was the love of his life, and I know it broke him when she died, leaving him with a young baby to look after.

Cancer took Mom when I was 4 years old. Being so young, I don't really have many memories of her, which is the hardest thing. The brothers in the club all loved her. Angel was the 'Mom' of the club. Looking after all the men and making sure the clubhouse was run as it should be. She was spicy and sweet, as my dad says. The brothers adored her.

They will tell me stories of a free-spirited angel who could melt any hardened heart with just her smile and then throw you a whole load of sass while still looking all innocent. Dad said Carrie reminds him of Mom, and Mom would have loved her. That lets me know Carrie is it for me.

The sun is starting to rise over the trees, and soon we will need to head back. Not wanting to break from this moment but knowing soon we will need to get back to real life.

However, this is only the beginning, as no way in hell am I letting her go now. She's my future, her and Johnny.

Wolf smacking me on the back brings me back to the present.

"Come on, son," is all he says.

He guides me back to the woods and our bikes. The ride back to the clubhouse helps clear my head a little, so I can focus.

Arriving at the clubhouse, I can see we're the last to get back. Walking through the main room toward church has an eerie quiet to it. Going into church, the brothers are all quiet. Taking our places, Prez begins.

"I've already briefly told the brothers what you told me on the phone. Reck, can you send the photos you took to the printer, so we can see what we're working with."

Nodding to Reck, he fiddles with his phone for a while, getting frustrated. With a smirk, Wire goes to help him, mumbling about stupid technology, breaking the atmosphere in the room a little.

Once the pictures are printed, Wire hands them to Prez. We all sit patiently while Prez looks over the photos. I'm watching his face for any emotion to tell me what he's thinking, but that's one of his strong points—the man shows no emotion at times.

Prez starts to hand the pictures out to all the brothers.

"Prez, this is serious shit. I mean, this is someone who is highly trained and knows what they are doing. Saw fucked up shit like this while I was servicing," Sarg confirms.

He was Special Forces, so the fucker should know what he's talking about.

"My suggestion is to place surveillance on the place. This fucker is going to come back."

Prez seems to be taking in what Sarg suggests. After all, he's our security expert.

"I agree. I want you and Wire to work together to set that up, take who you need with you. Once we have more information, we will meet again to plan our next step. What we found today alters how we proceed with finding Carrie."

His eyes find Reck and me straight away.

"We're not giving up! We just need to step carefully. Wire, do some more digging on the property. Stay close and stay together."

Prez slams the gavel down to end church.

CHAPTER SEVEN

CARRIE

After his little mind games, he leaves me locked in the basement. Part of the basement is walled off to create a room for his fun. Fun! That really is a joke.

Torture is more like it. I can see in his eyes how much it turns him on, trying to break me and causing me pain. Well, fuck him if he thinks I'm giving in. I have too much to fight for.

Sitting on the bed, I've really got nothing else to do but think. What more can he do to me? He's already hurt me in more ways than I could imagine. The mind games are the worst as you don't know where his evilness would take you next.

The rumble of bikes draws me out of my head. I jump up, then wish I hadn't. My body aches from being abused, and pain radiates all over. Slowly I work my way over to the boarded-up window. I try to see through a few gaps in the slats that are across the window. I would know the sound of Harleys anywhere.

A sliver of hope begins to rise inside me. Maybe the club had found me. I hope they are looking for me, but really, who knows. I try not to think about it too much, as to be honest, they have more than likely moved on. Does Johnny even remember me? Is he happy? I miss my brother so much. When it comes to Jason, I can't think of him as it hurts too much.

The Harleys start up again, and the noise fades into the distance. My body sags as I make my way back over to the bed and plop down. Head in my hands, I feel my resolve wavering. At the worst possible time, I hear his footsteps on the stairs. Fuck not now! Steeling myself for when he gets here, I straighten my spine and look bored.

The door to my prison opens, and he swaggers in.

"Well, little pet, it seems we might have had company. Had some bikers searching the empty property across the way. So close yet so far." He grabs my chin to make me look at him. "You're a biker trash whore." He spits at me. "So far, I've been easy on you," he snarls.

Easy. He really is in a world of his own if he thinks what he'd done to me already was going easy. His eyes run over my body, and I fight the urge to attempt to cover myself.

"You really have grown into a beautiful woman Carrie. But you're still a whore, and whores love it rough."

He traces his fingers down my neck, along my collarbone, and slowly between my breasts. I want to shiver in disgust, but don't, as I know this will turn him on. An evil smirk appears across his face as if he knows what I'm thinking.

"Don't worry, Pet, I'll break you slowly."

He laughs maniacally as I feel the pinch of the needle in my arm. Staring into his pure evil eyes, the world goes black.

My body feels heavy as I start to wake up. I don't want to alert him that I'm awake, so I try to keep my body as still as possible while I try to work out where I am. Thinking I might still be in the basement, I know I'm upright. Assessing my body, I now know

I'm naked, and my arms appear to be tied to something. I can also feel something hard under me, so I'm half-sitting, half perched onto something wooden with my legs tied, so they are open. Suddenly ice-cold water is thrown over me, making me gasp and splutter. His crazy laugh rings out around me.

"Wakey, wakey, my little pet."

Shaking the water from me, I take a minute to look around. I appear to still be in the basement, but fuck how long have I been out? He's managed to change the basement into some sort of torture chamber from hell. Looking up and down my body, I'm attached to what seems like a half chair, half cross.

"Ahh, I see you admiring my work of art. I created this masterpiece as it gives me access to every part of you without you being able to move."

The smile on his face shows how much pride he has in creating this torture device.

"Don't worry, Pet. I'll go easy on you at first."

He trails his fingers over my breasts and down my stomach.

"I told you I was going to enjoy breaking you. It is going to be so rewarding once you're fully mine," he purrs.

The look in his eyes scares me down to my bones. He's always been abusive, but he had never gone this far before. I can see it in his eyes that he really isn't going to hold back. Turning my head, I notice the camera. Fuck! Oh, hell no! Noticing where I'm looking, he grins.

"Yes, my little pet, people will pay big money to see beautiful women like you be broken."

Fuck, shit, damn, this can't be happening. I knew it was going to get worse, but not this much. My breathing becomes erratic as I desperately pull at my restraints, trying to free myself or even just loosen them. I need to get away from him or at least be able to defend myself.

Turning his back on me, he walks over to the table set up on the left side of the room with what looks like different devices on it. Humming a little tune to himself, he slowly picks each item up and inspects it, all while still humming that haunting little tune. God, if this were one of those stupid horror movies, it would be creepy. But for some reason, all I do is try to work out where I have heard the tune before.

What is wrong with me? I should be scared, should fear what comes next. But I don't. I mean, seriously, what more could he do to me?

As he finishes inspecting all the items on the table, he picks up a metal wheel with a spike on the end. It looks similar to a pizza cutter, but instead of a solid circle, it has spikes. With a grim look on his face, he walks over to me.

"This device is called a pinwheel and is designed to cause a pleasurable pain. I want to start you off slowly."

He starts to move the wheel slowly on the side of my left breast. The slight pain of the pins pushing into my sensitive flesh is bearable. Moving to the other side, he does the same to the other breast. After trying it in different areas, such as the inside of my thighs and also the bottom of my feet, it has me feeling a little worried. The pain is not what you would call painful, and I can see why people would use this during sex and enjoy it. However, this is not for me.

"I can see my little pet is starting to enjoy this. Are you wet for me, little pet?" I can feel his breath in my ear as he whispers to me. "Maybe I should check to see how much my pet is enjoying my little game."

His fingers trace down my collar bone, across the top of my breast, and down my stomach before dipping between my legs. Watching his face, I see the pleasure overtake his features as he finds my core and his fingers slipped inside of me. I know that this is my body's natural response and that I'm not enjoying his touch. I chant this in my head just to try to keep me from breaking.

"Oh, little pet, you're making me so proud. I feel how much pleasure I'm causing you. You love my touch."

The idea of loving what he's doing to me makes my stomach roll, and I fight not to be sick. He moves away from me and back to the table. It takes everything in me not to turn my head to see what he's doing. I keep my head up and stare straight at the wall.

"Now, now, little pet, show the camera how much you want this."

I feel his hands on my nipples, and something cold touches them. I can't help the flinch as the cold metal touches me. Catching my face, he smirks at me. I feel the metal clamps on my nipples as he tightens them, just enough to where it's uncomfortable. Thinking this is not so bad, he reaches for another clamp and connects this to my clit. The pain is more than the pinwheel, but still just as bearable. I'm beginning to think this is less about causing me pain and more about him having control. He moves over to a machine next to the table with wires coming from it. He connects the wires to the clamps.

"Do you know what this machine is, little pet?"

I refuse to talk as I know my voice will come out a little shaky.

"Well, little pet, this machine is used in electro convulsive therapy. Think of the volts that will pass through your body."

I can feel my panic start to bubble up. He moves over to the machine and starts it up. I feel my fingers dig into the restraints as I prepare myself.

"Don't worry, my little pet, we will start small...at first."

He moves the camera so it is now in front of me, and can see everything. I feel the first little shock, and my body jumps. Throwing my head back, I squeeze my eyes shut. The first shock is bad, but okay. I've got this! I keep telling myself I've got this. I will not give in. He cannot break me.

The next shock is stronger than the first, causing my body to shake, and I bite down on my tongue to stop me from screaming out. I can taste the blood in my mouth.

The third shock is worse, and my body convulses. His evil laugh can be heard all around me. The fourth is my undoing, and I cannot hold the scream that is ripped from my throat. By the fifth shock, the pain is unbearable, and my world goes black.

Everything feels heavy and painful when I try to move. As I slowly start to come around more, I can feel a hand on my head, slowly and gently stroking my hair. It feels comforting and nice. Trying to open my eyes, the bright light makes me close them again, and I respond with a groan.

"Beau, switch the main light off, please. Carrie? Are you with me?"

Opening my eyes again, the room now has a soft glow to it from the lamp.

"I'm here," I croak as my throat feels dry and sore.

"I'll get you some water," a little voice says. My heart breaks knowing my son is seeing me like this. I should be protecting him. He comes back over to the bed and places the straw against my lips. Meeting his eyes, I can see the hurt and worry in them. This only cements my decision. Taking a sip of the cold water, instantly, my throat feels better.

"Thank you, baby. I love you."

His eyes meet mine, and all I can see is sadness.

"I love you too, Momma," he kisses my cheek.

A tear slowly works its way down my cheek.

"Agnes, it's time," I say while I'm feeling brave enough.

"No, Carrie. He needs you."

I need him too, but I need him safe more.

"Agnes, it's getting worse. You didn't see the look in his eyes. It's not going to get any better. This needs to happen now. We have everything planned."

Agnes and I had planned that if anything were to happen to me or the abuse got to a certain point, she would take Beau and run.

"Come here, son," I reach my hand out for him.

"You and Agnes are going to go on a little trip. Remember what I told you about your daddy?"

Beau looks at me with an intense stare that is an exact copy of his father's.

"I remember, Daddy and my granddaddies' all ride motorcycles and are in a club. Daddy loves me with all his heart."

Pride swells in my chest. I had made sure my son knew if his daddy could, he would love him with all he had, as that is the kind of man he is.

"Agnes is going to take you to see your daddy. Promise me you'll be a good boy and do everything they say?"

With a small tear, he nods his head.

"Who's going to look after you, Momma?"

The pain in his voice is my undoing. Reaching for him, I hold him to me as tightly as possible.

"Momma will be just fine, baby." Kissing his forehead, my hands cup his face. "I love you to the moon and back," I whisper.

"I love you to the stars and more," he replies back.

After a few moments, I release him.

"Go now, Agnes."

Agnes starts to pack and retrieve the emergency escape bag we'd packed when Beau was born. It has everything we would need to get Beau to safety. I really had hoped we would never have to use it. Grabbing hold of Agnes' arm as she passes me, I say, "Agnes, in the bag, is a letter for Jason. Please make sure he gets it."

She gives me a knowing smile.

"Of course, sweetie," she says, patting my hand.

She really is the mother I never had. Hugging me tightly, she whispers, "I love you."

I hold her a little tighter. "I love you too. You've been the mom I always wanted."

Moving toward the bags, she gets ready to leave.

"Be a good boy Beau and remember how much I love you."

My words falter as I try not to cry. This is killing me. The pain I feel inside my chest as I watch them leave is unbearable. Part of me knows this is for the best, and I need to do whatever it takes to keep him safe. He's all I have left in the world, and I will keep him safe. I know Jason and the club would look after him. The room suddenly feels so big and cold, so I curl up into a ball as my tears start to fall. This is the only time I'll allow myself to break. He'll never get this from me.

CHAPTER EIGHT

JOKER

No one has ever accused me of being patient. I'm restless and can't keep still. Tank takes pity on me, and we spar in the club's gym at the clubhouse. I need something to distract me from going off the deep end. All I can think about is that torture room we found and praying to God my girl has not been anywhere near that room. I need to keep my mind from going to these dark places.

Waiting for Wire to come up with more information is excruciatingly painful, and it is taking all of my willpower not to go off on my own. I know I need my brothers help to find her and get her home safely, but that doesn't mean my heart is listening. I need to think about this all logically and not go off half-cocked, only to get myself killed. I'm no good to anyone if I'm dead.

Getting my head back in the game, I continue to work the bag. I'm taking all of my frustration out with every punch. Hearing the gym door open, BJ makes his way over to me.

"How're you doing, son?" he asks as he grabs a chair.

Stopping my pace, I grab the bag and rest my head against it while I catch my breath to form words. I can feel the sweat pouring off me and how heavy my arms feel. I must have really been lost in my head.

"Don't get lost in your head," BJ confirms after a few moments of silence. It's as if he can read my thoughts.

"I'm trying Prez, it's harder than you think not to go there. You saw that room," I say, closing my eyes and taking a deep breath.

With a deep sigh and slap on my shoulder, he replies, "I know, kid, but keep it contained. We will get her back."

Just as he's about to leave the room, a prospect comes through the door.

"Prez, do we have anyone called Jason here? There is a woman at the gate with a kid asking for him."

Turning to Prez, I raise my eyebrow puzzled.

"Get cleaned up, and I'll see what's happening." Prez leaves with the prospect.

Quickly heading to the locker room, I jump in the shower, making fast work of sorting myself out. I'm the only Jason at this clubhouse. None of the other brothers or prospects is called Jason that I know of. So, this woman must be someone who either knew me as a kid or knows someone who knew me as a kid. Otherwise, they would know my road name.

Making my way outside, I can see no one at the gate, so I head into the clubhouse. Seeing the prospect from the gate, I nod to him

"Prez is in church, said to send you in."

Nodding my thanks, I head for church. Stopping at the doors, I take a deep breath and try to calm my heart that feels like it's beating so fast it could leap from my chest at any moment. I have a feeling that whatever is on the other side of the door is going to be life changing. Taking another deep breath, I knock on the door.

"Come in," Prez shouts.

I push the door open and walk in.

Prez is sitting at the head of the table, and turning to his left, I notice a woman sitting there.

"You, I've seen you near the compound recently."

She slowly nods her head. I knew I wasn't going crazy and seeing things. It's then I notice a boy sitting next to her, and the bottom drops out of my world. He's the spitting image of me.

My eyes find Prez, and he nods. Well, fuck! I grab a chair and slowly lower myself into it. I can't take my eyes off of the boy. His face is turned down a little, and his eyes don't meet mine. Taking another breath, I look at the woman

"What's going on?" Stupidest question I could ask.

I actually want to smack myself in the head. I just don't want to say it out loud. My eyes drift back to the boy, and he finally looks at me. Connecting with his eyes, all the breath leaves my body, and one word falls from my lips, "Carrie!"

He has the bluest eyes I have only ever seen once in my life, and they belong to my girl.

Prez coughs to get my attention. I begrudgingly move to look at him.

"This lady's name is Agnes, and the boy is Beau. She's told me her story, but I'm going to let her tell you. Just hear her out and keep your mind calm," he says firmly. Nodding my understanding, I look to the woman, Agnes.

She gives me a small smile and starts her story by handing me a letter. I instantly know the writing. With shaking hands, I open the envelope and start to read.

By the end of the letter, I can feel the tears streaming down my face. Placing the letter on the table, I look to my son. Fuck, I have a son. He also has tears streaming down his face. Getting up from my chair, I can see the pain on his face.

Does he think I don't want him?

He was born from the love Carrie and I share. I turn as if I'm heading for the door, and I hear his intake of breath. He thinks I'm leaving him. I make my way around the table and drop down in front of him.

He slowly turns to face me. Raising my hand, he flinches, and rage powers through me. Whoever had caused my son to fear will die a slow and painful death. My protective father instinct kicking in already. I smile as I don't want to scare him and gently wipe away the tears with my finger.

"I'll never raise my hand to you, and I promise no one will ever hurt you again . . . Son."

The last part comes out on a choke. The next minute I'm on the floor, and Beau is on my knee. I wrap my arms around him and hold him as tight as I can without hurting him.

I can hear soft sobs. I look at Agnes as she sits there and softly cries.

"Thank you, Agnes, for looking after and protecting my girl and my son. You're family, and we will look after you."

Nodding to Prez, he smiles.

"How old is the boy?" Prez asks.

"Beau, his name is Beau," I correct.

God, the name hits me. Carrie and I used to love watching *Smokey and the Bandit* and joked once that if we ever had children, I would name them after the Bandit.

"He'll be ten years old soon," Agnes confirms.

Doing the math quickly in my head, I figure out he was conceived on Carrie's birthday. The memory of that night is cemented in my brain forever and was the best night of my life for more than one reason now.

Looking at Prez, he nods.

"I'll get the girls together to go get clothes, bedding, and anything else he might need. He'll need a bed too."

Still clinging to me, I lift him up. He's so light. I need to get a proper meal in him.

"Come on, champ. Let's get some food in you. What's your favorite?"

"Jason. Beau hasn't had many experiences. When it came to food, we ate what we could. He doesn't have a favorite like a normal child," Agnes confirms my worst fears.

"Thank you, Agnes. I think we will need to talk more later if that's okay. I have a lot of questions. But first, my son needs me."

I turn to look at my son in my arms. "Come on, champ, let's see what we can find in the kitchen that you might like to try. You can have anything you want."

Walking into the kitchen, I sit Beau down on the counter and turn toward the fridge.

"Right, my boy, what do you like the look of?" I ask, opening the fridge wide so he can look.

His eyes take in the whole fridge, and he looks down at his hands. Moving over to him, I gently lift his chin up.

"You can pick anything and everything you like. I understand you weren't allowed to before, but I promise you will never be denied food again."

His eyes still look sad, but he nods. He understands me. He looks back over to the fridge and seems to be closely inspecting each item. Pointing at a covered dish, "What's that?" he asks with a shaky voice.

"Good choice! That is the best pasta you will ever taste. Come on, let's try some."

Taking the bowl out of the fridge, I warm 2 plates up. Sitting at the breakfast bar, I pick up my knife and fork. Looking over to Beau, I can see him staring at the cutlery.

"You use a knife and fork before?"

Lifting his head to me, he gives me a strange look.

"I have, but usually I have to wait to be told when I can eat. He likes to eat first."

Rage ripples through me. I have to fight the urge to lose my shit. I'm going to need to watch any angry outbreaks in front of Beau.

"Well, son, here you don't need to wait. The minute the food's in front of you, eat. It's en masse here. You have many uncles who are all going to love you and spoil you, but also they will protect and care for you."

The most amazing smile lights up his face. Its breathtaking, fuck I'm already a sap for the kid. Knowing he was born from Carrie and me is amazing, but also guts me. I'm devastated I had missed him growing and being born. I'd missed so many firsts, but I need to focus on all the firsts I have to come, especially if he's not had a normal childhood.

I pull my phone from my pocket, and I text Prez. Hoping the girls haven't gone to get his stuff yet. I feel this might be a bonding father-son moment. Prez confirms they haven't, so I let him know I want to take the boy to Target. We would pick out his entire bedroom and kids' stuff together.

He agrees and lets me know he's thinking of moving my room to one further down the hall, so it's away from the noise, but also has an adjoining room so Beau can have his own space. It's a perfect idea. The prospects would get on with that while we're out.

Once we've finished eating, and Beau is wearing more sauce than is on his plate, which makes me chuckle, I say, "Right then, kid, I'm guessing you don't really have a lot of stuff?"

He looks down. Christ, this kid is killing me with the sad faces.

"How do you feel about your own room, right next door to mine? We can decorate it and fill it with everything you choose and like?"

His little face lights up, and he looks so excited. Chuckling, I collect our plates and put them in the dishwasher while grabbing a towel to wipe his face. Taking him by the hand, we leave the kitchen and head outside. As we get closer to my truck, I see my Pops and Tank, so I divert to speak with them.

"Who do we have here?" Pops asks with a confused look on his face.

"Yeah, so not really had a chance to fill you both in, but this is Beau, mine and Carrie's son."

The shocked look on both their faces makes Beau move behind my legs.

"He's not had it great. I'll fill you both in more later, but he's a little shy and timid."

Pops is still staring at him, but Tank crouches low and holds his hand out to Beau.

"Hey there pal, I'm your uncle, Tank. You and I are going to be great friends, and we can get into all sorts of mischief."

Beau moves from behind my legs, and his little fingers run over the string bracelet on Tank's wrist.

"Scott," says his little voice.

Holy fucking shit!

Tank falls to his ass on the ground, and Beau jumps into his arms, and he holds him tight. Tank looks up at me with hurt and disbelief on his face.

Carrie had made that bracelet for him when we were kids, and he's never taken it off. Clearly, Carrie has told our son all about his uncle Scott.

"You know me?" Tank asks slowly.

Beau backs away and returns to hiding behind my legs. I place my hand on his head, hoping to reassure him a little. His head peeks back around my legs, and he nods.

"Momma told me stories from when she was younger and the adventures, she went on with Daddy, Scott, and Johnny. Scott and Johnny are my uncles. You have my uncle's bracelet, so you must be my uncle," he confirms in his quiet little voice, shaking like he's afraid to speak. Beau being afraid to speak and hiding, needs to stop. Tank seems to be in another world as he stares at Beau as if he cannot believe Carrie had told him all about what we got up to.

"Okay, so we're off to get little dude everything he needs," I declare.

With my hand on Beau's shoulder, I start to guide him toward the truck.

"I'll tag along," Tank says as he jogs toward my truck.

I give him a chin lift as we all get into the truck.

The drive to the nearest Target isn't too far, and the whole way there, Beau has his face pressed against the window taking everything in. All too soon, we're in the parking lot. Watching Beau in the mirror, his eyes are wide.

"Son, you ever been to a store like this before?"

He slowly shakes his head while still taking everything in.

"Okay, so this place sells everything you could ever need. We're going to get you some clothes and stuff for your new bedroom."

Jumping out of the truck, I open his door for him.

"It's going to be busy in there, lots of people, but that's okay. Uncle Tank and I will be with you, and nothing will happen. If you see anything you like, let one of us know, and we will get it for you. Okay?"

Tank and I each grab a cart and head into the store with Beau between us. We head straight for the clothes, grabbing him jeans, underwear, tops, and pajamas. Tank finds a pair of kid's biker boots, making me smile.

"Look, dude, same as your dad's and mine."

Beau has a massive smile, he's still timid, but luckily, it's not too busy, so he's been okay. He tries a couple of pairs of boots on until we find the right size. Now we know his size, I can order him some decent footwear.

A couple of loud kids run past us, followed by a harassed looking mom shouting at the kids. Beau's hidden between the carts, trying to make himself really small, frightened by the sudden noise and movement.

Fuck, I knew this was going too well. Tank gets down to his level again and takes his bracelet off.

"Beau, you're safe now. We're going to make sure of it. I want you to have this."

He ties the bracelet onto Beau's wrist.

"Now you always have something that reminds you of your momma and know we're always with you, keeping you safe."

Jesus, the smile that lights up his face when Tank gives him that bracelet, I'm glad he came with us. Beau seems to calm down and we manage to fill the carts with everything the kid needs, plus a few other bits such as toys. I get him an Xbox and all the age-appropriate games I could find too.

I know he's ten years old, but he's not a normal ten. He's never been to school or around normal kids his age. Thinking maybe a trip to some places other kids his age go, like the park and stuff is in order.

Making it back to the compound with the truck piled high with stuff, we get Beau set up in the bar with his new Lego while I get the prospects to haul all the crap we bought into our rooms. I go to start unpacking, but Pip has beaten me to it.

"Go spend time with your son. I got this," she shoos me out of the room.

Prez's ol' lady is one of a kind. She's sweet, kind, and soft. But she can put men four times her size in their place with just a look and a few choice words. Making my way back downstairs, I sit and build the Lego with Beau. Watching the concentration on his face is sweet. His little tongue sticks out as he's thinking and working out how it all fits together. He might not have been to school, but the kid's smart. Pops and Reck join us on the sofas in the common room.

"Beau, come here a minute, please. Got some important people I want you to meet."

With a little pout that makes me chuckle, he comes over and sits next to me.

"Beau, this is Bull and Reck. They're your granddads. Bull is my dad, and Reck is your mom's dad."

He looks at me for a second and then slowly turns to look at them. Reck's face is awash with so many emotions it's hard to get a read on them all.

"You look just like your dad, Beau. I'm Grandpa Bull." He holds his hand out for Beau to shake, which he does, making me smile. The more he seems to be around the compound and the brothers, the more he seems at ease.

"Beau, I'm Grandpa Reck." He opens his arms a little as if he wants a hug. Beau looks at me as if he's asking if it's okay. I give him a little nod, and he hugs Reck. Reck gets choked up and seems to hold him tighter.

"Beau, you also have an uncle named Johnny. He's your mom's brother. But you can think of every man here as your uncle. They will all care for and protect you."

Reck is not wrong, as we've been playing Lego in the common room, all the brothers have been stopping by to say hi and introduce themselves. Some had even played Lego with us for a bit. I'm really hoping having everyone around will help Beau settle in. Bull smacks me on the back.

"You doing good, kid? We have church, but Pip is going to watch Beau."

I knew we would have to meet at some point, especially with the new information we have on Carrie. I can feel that we're close to getting my girl back. I know it's not going to be easy once we do, but I'm prepared. Pip appears from the rooms.

"Beau's bedroom is all sorted. Beau, do you want to come have a look while your dad talks with the brothers?" she says, holding her hand out to Beau.

"Yes, please." He jumps up all excited and then suddenly stops. "Where is Agnes?" He looks to me for the answer.

"Agnes has her own room across from yours. She's been lying down."

He looks as if he's thinking this over.

"We can see if she's awake when we've looked at your new room," Pip assures him.

That seems to be the right answer, and they head for the bedrooms while we make our way into church. Taking my seat, I wait for BJ to start.

"Okay, so we've had a development in the search for Carrie. A woman by the name of Agnes turned up at the compound early this morning with a little boy in tow. The boy, Beau, is nine years old and is Carrie and Joker's son."

He takes a minute to let that sink in, and the brothers all congratulate me.

"Agnes confirmed that she and the boy have been with Carrie this whole time. However, she and

Carrie had an agreement that if it got too dangerous, she would escape with Beau and bring him here to safety. It was too risky for Carrie to leave too."

"What has this Agnes woman told us about Carrie?" Reck is the first to speak.

"It's not good, brother. She's alive, but we need to figure out a way to get Carrie out. The man who's keeping her has stepped up the abuse, and it's getting worse. Agnes said when she left, Carrie was not in a great condition." He looks at me with sympathy.

"Wire, I need you to do your thing and find any trace of Carrie anywhere."

Giving the Prez a confused look, he sighs.

"Agnes mentioned Carrie is not the first girl this man has had. He usually films what he does to them for fetish sites and also dark web sicko sites. He's never done this to Carrie before, so we might be able to stop it before it gets to that point."

I feel sick. I feel like my insides want out. He had filmed what he's done to her so other sickos can get off on it. For the first time, I'm scared to bring her home. She's going to need a lot of help to come to terms with what's happened to her and move on with her life.

Reck's chair slamming into the wall pulls me from my head. He storms out of church. Bull gets up and follows him out.

"I'll get on it now, Prez," Wire confirms as he leaves.

The brothers all file out of church which leaves me, Tank, and Prez still in the room.

"I know that must have been hard to hear, Joker. You doing okay?"

Shaking my head, I drop it into my hands. It's a lot of information he had dropped on me, and now there's not only me to consider. I feel a hand on my shoulder.

"We're all here for you, son. You're not alone, and neither is Beau or Carrie. We will get through this as a family."

I honestly wish I could believe him. But a part of me is afraid of what we would find once we found Carrie. It's a lot for one person to go through, and now she had lost her reason to keep going. She would have pulled herself up for Beau, because that's the type of person she is. I had watched her do it for Johnny when we were younger. She always put him and me before herself.

"Let's go spend some time with your kid while we wait," Tank mutters as he makes his way out of church. Following behind him into the common room, Beau is sitting with Pip doing some sort of puzzle.

"Hey Beau, wanna come spend some time in the family room with your dad and me?" Tank holds his hand out for Beau, not really giving him a choice.

"Okay," he says with a smile.

Making our way into the family room, we decide maybe a movie would be a good place to start. Choosing a movie that isn't too babyish for him, we get comfy and watch *Toy Story*.

A few hours later, we're on *Toy Story 3*, and Beau loves it. He keeps copying Woody and Buzz. His impressions are spot on, making us laugh. He then does an impression of Tank, which is hilarious as he tries to get his voice real deep. This kid is a born entertainer when he feels comfortable.

"What's all the laughing?" Prez asks from the door, with Reck and Bull behind him. Beau instantly stops and comes closer to me.

"It's okay. They won't hurt you," I reassure him.

"Kid is a genius at impressions," Tank tells the others.

"Beau, show them your impression of Tank," I encourage.

"Oh, this I gotta see," Bull says with a laugh and gets comfy. Reck also sits.

Prez stays near the door and watches. Beau seems to be looking right at him.

"Come on, Beau, I wanna see too," Prez says softly.

Beau smiles and does his impression causing them all to laugh loudly.

"Do me, do me!" Bull says. Beau gives it his best, and he's bloody close.

"What about me?" Prez asks.

Beau hesitates and looks at me. I give him a slight nod. He puffs his chest out, trying to make himself bigger than he is, holds his arms on his hips and says, "Goddamn idiots."

His voice is spot on, but his whole impression has us losing our shit. Reck lets out a stomach-holding laugh, and Prez is laughing. A feminine giggle comes from the doorway, and Pip is standing there watching us. Coming into the room, she ruffles Beau's hair and kisses his forehead.

"Born entertainer."

Beau looks so proud of himself. He carries on his impressions, and more brothers join us and ask him to impersonate them too. He picks up all the traits of each brother quickly, which just makes it funnier, but also shows me he's always watching his surroundings and reading people. This seems to lift our spirits and is exactly what we need.

CHAPTER NINE

CARRIE

God, I miss my boy. I miss Agnes too. I know it was the right decision to send them away. The plan was always that I would go with them, but there was no way I could. The pain in my body would've meant holding them back. I needed to put Beau first. If they had made it to Jason and the Sons, then I know they would help get me free. Well, I hope to God they would help. When my dad went away, we didn't spend much time around them as Mom hated them. She had blamed them for Dad no longer being around. I did ask Bull a few times about my dad, but he wouldn't tell me. He just got this really sad look on his face and had told me it was 'club business.' He did tell me, though, that if my dad could be with me, he would be. I'd held onto that with all my heart. I'd loved my dad and was such a daddy's girl.

I often think about him and Johnny. Where are they now? Are they okay? Are they together?

Dad had taught me so much. He taught me how to protect myself and Johnny. When he went away, Bull took over a little. He taught me how to shoot a gun.

He really helped me feel like I wasn't missing out on not having my dad around. Plus, Jason was always with Johnny and me when he wasn't at the club with Bull.

Did Jason end up following in his dad's footsteps? Is he now a brother? He used to always talk about how he wanted to prospect when he was old enough. When he had talked about the Sons and the brotherhood, he had such pride in his voice.

Living as part of an MC is not an easy, romantic life like you see on television. It's gritty, dirty, and soul-destroying, but it's also wonderful. The sense of family and love they have for each other is more than anyone outside the club can understand. These men may seem rough and scary, but you only need to worry if you cross them. Being loved and cared for by these men is truly inspiring. They love with their whole hearts and are as loyal as they come. I miss the friendships and watching them interact together as one huge family who would always have your back. It is this notion that I hold onto as it means they would come for me. I just need to stay strong until then.

The door opens, and he walks in.

"You disappoint me, pet, they got away, and you let them. You will be punished."

His voice has a violent edge to it that makes my skin crawl. This is not good. I knew he wouldn't be happy that they had managed to slip past him, but I honestly thought he wouldn't care. I should have known he would take it bad.

His hand grips my chin hard between his fingers and moves my head to look at him.

"Your first video has been a huge success. You appear to be popular."

Knowing sick men have watched videos of what he's done to me and gotten off on it makes me sick to my stomach.

"I'm looking forward to your next starring movie."

Oh, fuck! Yeah, this is not good. I feel the needle enter my arm and the cold spread through me.

Looking into his eyes, I can see the pain he's going to cause me. The drug kicks in, and my eyes feel heavy. I try to fight the heavy feeling, but do not succeed as it drags me under.

Waking up, I can see I'm back in his fun room as he refers to it. My arms are chained to the ceiling, and my legs are chained to the floor spread wide. I'm completely naked. Looking around, I can see the table with his toys to the side, and a camera is set up again in front of me. Moving my head, I can see another camera is set up behind me.

He enters the room. However, unlike normal, he's wearing a mask that covers the top half of his face and hair. Seeing the confusion on my face, he laughs.

"Can't have myself being identified. We're going to have some fun today."

He walks to the table picking up the remotes and clicks the cameras on. He moves back over to me, stroking his finger along my cheek and down my throat. Wrapping his fingers around my throat, he slowly starts to squeeze. I can feel the air leaving my lungs. I start to struggle when it seems he's not letting go. This does nothing but make him smirk. Just as spots start to appear in my vision, he lets go, and I gasp for breath. I'm trying to suck as much air into my lungs as I can. His hand doesn't move away. Once I have my breath back, he starts all over again. Slowly squeezing until just before I would pass out, and then he lets go, so I gulp air in.

He does this a few times. I can see his erection through his jeans. This is turning him on so much. He loves holding this power over me. Once he's happy with the bruises I'm sure are on my neck, he moves away to the table. Hanging my head forward as I try to catch my breath, I feel the first strike of leather across my back, causing my head to fly back, and a groan escapes my mouth. I feel the leather hit my back again, but this time I know it is coming, and I bite down on my lip to stop the scream that is lodged in my throat.

"I'll make you scream," his voice whispers in my ear.

I hear the leather fly through the air before it strikes me across my back. Fuck, it's harder than the last, but I still manage to hold my scream in. He strikes me again, this time across my lower back. He's getting stronger with every strike, and I'm finding it difficult to hold my scream in.

The next strike has me losing my willpower, and a scream breaks free from my throat and echoes around the room. I can feel the trickles of blood trailing down my back and legs. My head hangs forward as I struggle to hold it up through the intense burning on my back. He continues to strike me a few more times, and each time a scream rips from me like a wounded animal. It's killing me that he broke me. He knew he would, and I'd fought as hard as I could, but I'm only human.

Tears run down my face. I feel his hand in my hair as he grabs a handful and yanks my head back, making me look into his twinkling eyes. He's really enjoying this.

He trails the tip of the whip handle along my jaw and to my lips.

"Suck," he demands as he forces the tip of the handle into my mouth.

"That's so beautiful, Pet. My cock would look perfect in that pretty little mouth of yours."

He moves away, removing the handle from my mouth.

Suddenly the chains holding my arms up jerk and start to lower me down until I'm practically kneeling on the wooden bench in front of me.

Gripping my hair again, he forces my lips open and inserts a metal contraption into my mouth to stop it from closing. It feels cold against my lips. Gripping my hair harder, he unbuttons his trousers and removes his hard cock. Moving me into position, he starts to push his cock into my mouth until he hits the back of my throat, making me gag. He then continues to fuck my mouth until tears are streaming down my face.

"Fuck, you feel so good. You're enjoying this, aren't you, Pet?"

He keeps thrusting into my mouth, and his grip is getting tighter in my hair. I can feel the roots pulling at my scalp to the point of pain.

He pulls out and removes the metal from my mouth. My jaw is aching, so I try to relieve it a little by moving it around as much as I can. The chains jerk again, and I'm moving up again until I'm back in the position I was before.

"You have pleased me, Pet," he coos.

God, I didn't want to please him. I don't want to give into him and make him happy. I want to fight. Feeling his hands on my body, I know what is coming next.

"As you have pleased me greatly, my pet, I'll allow you pleasure."

It's not pleasure. It's my body reacting. I had stopped trying to fight it a long time ago. Instead, I retreat into my head and ignore what he's doing to me. This is for his pleasure and the weird sickos who would watch the video. This is not for me.

I let my mind wander to a happy place, to the woods behind the clubhouse. If you follow the slightly hidden trail, you come to a clearing and a lake. It's so beautiful and peaceful. I imagine myself with Beau, watching him play in the water like a normal kid, while I relax in the sun on the bank. He would splash around in the shallow part. My dad and Johnny would be there too. I watch them play in the water with Beau. Beau jumping into the water from my dad's shoulders like he used to do with me when I was little. Then we would enjoy a picnic or a BBQ. BBQ is my favorite. I used to love going to the cook-outs at the compound. Playing and running around with all the other MC brats. The brothers would laugh at us as we would run riot around the compound. The old ladies relaxing in the sun and the few club bunnies that were around would be cooking the food. Even though they were bunnies, they were still part of the family. They were respectful and only went with single brothers. No drama was caused as BJ wouldn't allow it. He's a great Prez, or so my dad always said.

BJ and Pip are like the perfect couple. Everyone loved them. You could see how much they loved each other. Pip was always kind and soft, but don't mistake that as weakness. She could put a brother in his place with that fierce look she has and a few choice words.

I miss those days.

My body shaking brings me out of my head. He's lowering me to the floor and removing the cuffs from around my wrists and ankles. Stroking my hair slowly, he says, "You did so well, my pet. You're beautiful when you come."

My body shivers, and he smiles, thinking it's a good shiver.

Picking me up off the floor, he carries me from the fun room to my room. Placing me on the bed, he continues to stroke my hair.

"Rest now, my pet."

He leaves the room, closing the door behind him. I know I need to rest and reserve my energy. If I've pleased him, I know he won't let me rest long before he's back for more.

Letting my eyes drift close, sleep claims me.

I must have been asleep for a while as when I wake, the room is just starting to get dark. Taking stock of my body, I note where I hurt the most. Slowly moving from the bed to the mirror, I see the bruising around my throat, around my ankles, and wrists. There is bruising on my breasts and bite marks on my shoulders. I turn around to take a look at my back. Wincing as I move, I look over my shoulder. Big red welts are sliced across my back. At some point, he'd came in and cleaned my back and put salve on the broken skin.

It shocks me more that he had taken the time to care for me. Usually, it was Agnes who had cleaned me up.

Making my way to the bathroom, I do my business which is uncomfortable, to say the least. I make a hot drink with the mini kitchen in my room and a snack. Curling up in the chair by the window, I watch the last of the sun go down. Flicking the lamp on, I think about Beau and what he is doing now.

Is he thinking of me? Are we looking at the same sky?

"Love you to the moon and back, baby boy," I whisper as a tear escapes down my cheek.

I really hope he's safe. I'm aware of the shock it would be for Jason to learn he has a son. I just hope I still know him as well as I used to, and he takes Beau in with open arms. I hope he looks after and accepts Agnes too. She's been the mom I always wished I had. She was trapped here just as I was, but he had allowed her some freedom thinking she would never leave him. He was wrong, and she was just waiting for the right time. He really thought he had broken her enough that she wouldn't go against him. What a joke! Women are devious by nature. We plot and plan before we have our revenge. It will be when you least expect it. You see, women are stronger than men give them credit for. We're no longer the weaker sex that needs to be saved by a white knight like all the fairy tales. I want a dark knight who would sweep me off my feet and stand beside me while we fight our demons together.

Now that's a fairy tale!

The door to my room opens, and he walks in. God, what does he have planned for me now? He takes my hand and pulls me up from the chair and leads me over to the bed.

"I trust you feel rested, and your back is not too painful, my pet."

He's never asked me this before. He's never cared before about my health.

"Not too painful," I confirm.

He pulls the cord of my robe, releasing it and pushing it over my shoulders, so it pools around my feet. He's trailing his fingers down my arms and along my shoulders. Turning me so my back is to him, he gently traces his fingers over the marks on my back, causing a hiss to escape my lips. He then slowly and softly kisses each mark on my back. I hold myself as still as possible. His gentleness is freaking me out more than anything he's ever done. His finger glides along my sides and slowly moves to run along the underside of my breasts. Turning me to the side to face him, he lowers his head and lightly licks my nipple while his other hand finds my other breast, and he rolls my nipple between his fingers. "Lie down, my pet."

Doing as he says, I lie down on the bed. He climbs in next to me and continues to shower my breasts with attention.

"You're so beautiful, pet. You're even more beautiful than when you broke for me."

He kisses my nipples before slowly kissing further down. He stops just as he gets to my pelvis. His hand slides down between my legs and slowly enters me.

"You're so wet for me, my pet. I love how much you enjoy the pleasure I give you."

He's delusional. I know this is my body's natural response and has nothing to do with me enjoying anything. His hands on me make my stomach turn, and it's taking everything in me not to be sick on him. He moves off the bed and takes his trousers off. Joining me back on the bed, he moves between my legs and slowly pushes into me.

This whole thing feels like sensual lovemaking. I know better. He's not capable of love. He's a monster, pure evil. Love is something he has no idea about. He can't love. Otherwise, how could he do the things he does.

Once he's finished, he curls himself around me as if we're some couple and kisses my shoulder. "You have pleased me greatly, my pet."

After a few minutes of lying here, he gets up and dresses. With one last look at me and a smile on his face, he leaves me in peace.

Getting up, I head for the shower as I want to remove all traces of him from me. I scrub my skin until it's raw. I still feel dirty. I think a part of me will always feel dirty when it comes to the things he's done to me. But it does not define who I am. I'm not a victim, and he'll not affect my life. One day I'd be free, and he wouldn't be.

Crawling back into bed after I've changed the sheets, I curl up into a ball and dream of the life I wish I had with Beau.

CHAPTER TEN

JOKER

It's been over a week since Beau came to the compound, and every day, he seems more and more comfortable with everyone. The guys love him and are always having him do impressions to entertain them. He's mine and Tank's little mascot, following us around. He's spending time in the garage and struck up a friendship with Wrench.

Wrench even bought him his own mini tool kit to keep at the garage and a pair of coveralls with his name on them. The first time he wore them, he even wore them to bed. He loves them so much. He's a great kid, and I've loved getting to know him. Spending time with him has kept me calm while Wire and Webbie have been looking for Carrie.

Beau asks about his mom all the time, and I've promised him we're doing everything we can to bring her home to him. His favorite bedtime stories are when he has Tank and me telling him tales from when we were kids and what we had all got up to.

He's met Johnny and loves him. Johnny spends a lot of time playing with him. Reck bought him a replica Harley similar to my own. His eyes lit up when he gave it to him. He insisted we go for a ride together, so we rode around the compound. Beau riding his little electric bike and me on the real thing. Pip managed to snap a photo of us both which she had framed, and it is sitting on his nightstand. I have the same photo on mine too, next to the photo I have of Carrie and me.

Agnes seems to be settling in well. She's taken to cooking and cleaning for everyone, a little like a house mother as she's living at the compound. BJ gave her a room at the back, away from the noise. Pip also seems to have struck up a friendship with her, and the two are always found somewhere together. Agnes also seems to be getting close to Reck. I've noticed them spending time together.

I'm currently in the family room with Beau, and we're watching a Disney movie. We've been trying loads of different cartoons and kids' movies to see what he likes. *Jungle Book* is a favorite of his, and he sings along to the songs. *Charlie and The Chocolate Factory* is also a favorite, but what kid wouldn't love all that candy and chocolate?

Pip joins us to watch the movie, bringing popcorn with her.

"BJ's called church. I'll sit with him," she whispers to me.

Ruffling the kid's hair, I say, "I got church, Beau. Pip will watch with you. Be back soon."

He looks up, grinning at me, and cuddles into Pip as I leave and head into church.

Seems I'm the last one in and quickly take my seat. Looking around, all the brothers seem uneasy. Looking at BJ's face, I can tell what he's got to say is not good.

"Okay, Wire came to me today as he and his web friend have been hunting for any trace of Carrie they can find. About an hour ago, he came across a video that was uploaded on a fetish website."

Taking a deep breath, he lets what he just said sink in. A fetish website, what the fuck! This is not going to be good. I can feel it already.

"Wire and his friend are currently working to trace the link of who uploaded the video and where from. Hopefully, this will give us a location for Carrie."

The brothers all nod.

"What was the video?"

"Reck, I knew you or Joker would ask, but I'll warn you against seeing it."

I can't help myself. "Have you seen it?"

He lowers his head and lets out a sigh. I have my answer.

"Yes, I've seen it, and I wish I hadn't."

"I wanna see it. I wanna know what they've done to my baby girl so when we catch the sick fuck, I can make sure she has her revenge."

Prez nods his head like he understands. He presses a button, and the television on the wall behind him comes to life. Clear as day, I can see Carrie, her head is hanging down. She's strung to some device, but also looks like she's sitting too. She's naked and does not look good. I can feel the rage building inside of me. Prez presses play.

I watch the girl I love as she's electrocuted, and her body defiled while she's unconscious.

"Stop," Reck screams out, his head in his hands.

Unable to help myself, I stand and leave church. Heading straight for the bar, I grab the bottle of tequila and take a mouthful straight from the bottle. Feeling the burn run down my throat helps my rage. I take a few more swigs from the bottle and head for the family room.

Beau is playing some game, but I scoop him up and hold him close to me. Walking to the corner of the room where the big comfy chair is, I drop down in it holding Beau even closer. As if he senses what I need, he wraps his arms around me and holds me just as tightly. This is my undoing. Tears stream down my face. I bury my face in his neck and just hold him tight. This grounds me, having him in my arms. I'm not too man enough to admit seeing my girl like that broke my soul. At least she was unconscious and won't know the sick things he did to her, and I didn't see all of the video. I just couldn't stomach anymore. Reck joins us a little later and holds Beau the same way for a while. Then we sit together, the three of us watching a movie. Beau's head is on my chest, but he's holding Reck's hand and has his little feet touching him as if he's trying to comfort us both.

"Tank's in the gym beating the shit out of the bag," these are the first words Reck has spoken to me. His voice is a little more strained than normal, so I know he's still trying to rein himself in and get control of himself.

"It's hard on us all who love her," I tell him.

I knew this would affect Tank as much as it did us. He loves Carrie like a sister.

We sit in silence for a while longer, and Beau falls asleep. Lifting him carefully, I carry him to bed. On the way, Prez stops me.

"I know that was hard, son, and if I had my way, you wouldn't have ever seen your girl like that, but also, I think it will help us when we get her back to understand what happened so we can work out the best way to help her."

I know he's right, but it still kills me.

"Was that the only video?"

Placing his hand on my shoulder, he looks at me with a sadness I've never seen before.

"Wire just told me a new one was added a few minutes ago."

Dropping my head, I hold Beau a little tighter.

"I'll just put him to bed and be back in church."

Prez nods and heads back to church.

Making my way to Beau's room, I manage to get him in his pajamas and into bed. His face when he's asleep looks like an angel. I watch him sleep for a few minutes before I head back down to church.

Slowly taking my place, Tank catches my eye. He does not look like he's handling this well. His knuckles are bloody, and some attempt to patch them up was made but not well.

"Tank when we're done, have Doc look at your hands," Prez orders.

He just nods his head in understanding.

"Right, another video has been uploaded."

Fuck no. I'm not sure I can take another video like the last one.

The video appears on the screen and shows my girl strung up from the ceiling and the sick bastard with a mask covering his face whipping her. I can see the pain on her face, but she's not giving him the satisfaction of knowing she's in pain. Carrie is strong, and I feel so proud of her strength.

Looking over to Reck, I can see he's barely keeping it together. Suddenly the room is filled with the most harrowing scream. Reck is out of the chair, and the chair goes flying across the room into the television, just missing Prez. His whole body is vibrating with rage. A rage like no other, he's hulking out.

I know how he feels. That scream would live with me for the rest of my life.

Looking around the room, pain, rage, and clear desperation are showing on the face of every brother present.

"It's clear that video has affected us all greatly. If anyone needs to talk, my door is open."

Prez knows as men we keep a lot inside, but some things are good, healthy even, to talk about and not bottle up.

Just as everyone settles down, Wire comes into church.

"We have a possible location."

That gets everyone's attention. Laying a map and photos out on the table, he starts to explain that the videos were uploaded from a farmhouse a few towns over. The details fit what Agnes was able to describe for us.

"Get Agnes. NOW!" Prez yells, looking directly at Reck, who a few minutes later comes back with Agnes behind him, gripping his hand.

"You're not in trouble, Agnes. We need your help," Prez sooths.

Nodding her head, her body relaxes a little until she notices the pictures on the table. Her whole body tenses back up and then some. That's all we need to know. This is the place. Slowly she makes her way to the table and picks up a photo of the farmhouse.

"You found it?" her voice is shaky.

Reck instantly goes to her and wraps his arms around her waist and holds her close. Giving her the support she needs.

"Yes, we believe this is where Carrie might be," replies Prez.

Nodding her head, she looks to Reck.

"This is the house we were in. I escaped with Beau through the back and out through the woods to the main road, where we walked into town. We hid behind some shops on the main street until the bus came."

God, she went through so much to get my son to me safely.

"Okay, thank you, Agnes," said Prez.

Reck leads a shaking Agnes from church and returns a few moments later.

"Pip is with her," he confirms when he comes back.

"We need a plan. I've been looking at the surrounding area, and the aerial photos Wire has. We need to split into teams and cover each side of the property. That way, we can approach through the woods and have the element of surprise. Wire, can you tell if he has any surveillance around the property?" asks Tank.

Tank takes over. As Sergeant at Arms, this is his job, and he's the fucking best at what he does.

"Couldn't find any cameras, but that doesn't mean he doesn't have something within the woods," answers Wire.

"It's going to take me an hour or so to go over everything here and form a plan of attack."

Tank is thorough and won't risk brothers' lives.

"Okay, Tank, you come up with a plan, everyone else rest and make sure your weapons are ready to go in two hours. I'll get the prospects to gas up the vans. Meet back here in two hours." BJ makes the plan, and we all leave to get ready.

In my room, I make sure Beau is okay and then get to cleaning my guns and making sure I have enough ammo. I also go out to the shed and sharpen my knives. You can never be too careful.

Once I'm all set to go, I check on Beau one more time and see he's awake so I decide to spend some much-needed time with him. We play Xbox. He loves the Lego Batman game. He's really gotten into his Lego, so at least I know what to get him for his birthday and Christmas now.

Before long, it's time. Putting Beau back to bed, I read him a story or two until he's asleep. Kissing his forehead, I make my way into my room to get changed. Pip is going to keep an eye on him for me, so I find her in the kitchen and give her the monitor. I know he's old enough where he doesn't need a baby monitor, but the clubhouse is big, and we don't want him wandering around on his own during the night.

Heading into church, I take my place and wait for everyone else. Soon all the brothers are here. Tank takes the floor.

"We're splitting into four teams. Each team will take a side, and we will approach and survey first. On my signal, we will approach. If you're on the sides, stay outside and look for movement. Team One will go in the front, and Team Four will go in the back. Reck, Wrench, Angel, and Rafe will be on Team One. Bull, Joker, BJ, and I will be on Team Four. Striker and Sarg, I need you both in sniper positions in the trees, a corner each so you can see a side and the front, a side, and the back. Trader, Jackal, Wolf, and Youngblood will be Team Two, with Dog, Anchor, and Marvel on Team Three. Get your earpieces from Wire on the way out. You wait for my signal. You all know what to do."

Getting into our teams, we all jump in the waiting vans and head toward the location. It doesn't take us too long to get there. We park within the woods so the vans are hidden, but also so we can make a quick getaway if needed. Leaving the vans, we slowly make our way through the woods to the edge of the property. The moon is the only light, making it difficult to see through the woods. We get into position and wait. I hate fucking waiting. Striker and Sarg confirm they are in position and have eyes on the house.

"You see anything in your scopes?" asks Tank.

Both are in excellent vantage points to see movement within the house.

"Nope, looks deserted," replies Sarg.

"Same here, no movement and no lights on," says Striker.

"Okay, proceed with caution, watch your backs," warns Tank.

We start to make our way to the front of the house while Reck's team makes their way to the back of the house. We hover near the door waiting for the signal from Reck.

"In position, on my count, three, two, one, enter."

On enter, we kick the front door down with guns drawn and enter the house. The place is eerily quiet. We clear the living room and head into the kitchen. Meeting Reck and his team, he nods to say it's clear, and we head upstairs, and Team One clears the basement. I find a room that has a few kids' bits in it and also some female clothes. Seems this could have been Carrie and Beau's room. There is a lock on the outside of the door, which ignites the rage that has been slowly simmering all day. The sicko had locked my girl and son in this crappy room. Mold is growing up the walls, and it seems the window is locked. There is only one bed with just a cheap old sheet. As if they lived like this, the images running through my head of Carrie and Beau curled up on the lumpy ratty mattress, huddled together to keep warm, is breaking my heart. No wonder Beau loves his bed and starfishes on it when he sleeps.

Moving out of the room, I head down the hallway, Tank is in another bedroom, which looks much the same as the other, but this has no lock. However, you can see where one once was. The room also has female bits in it, so this must be Agnes' room. Her room is no better than Carrie's except, at some point, the lock has been removed. Stepping out, I try the room across the hall. This one is much different from the others. There's a large comfy bed with bedding on it, plus a large television. It's clean and miles better than the other rooms. This must be his room. Sick fucker let them live like animals while he had full luxury. All the rooms upstairs are clear. Back downstairs, we all meet in the kitchen.

"Place is clear, found a room in the basement where the videos were filmed. Fuck, seeing it in person, it's even more sickening," Bull confirms my fears.

"There is no one here," Tank says as Wolf shouts to us all from down in the basement. "Found a door with a tunnel."

Following Wolf, he leads us to what looks like a cupboard, but on closer inspection, has a false back that leads into an underground tunnel. Wolf, Tank, and I follow the tunnel while the others go back up to see if they find anything in the outbuildings. We seem to walk for a while before coming to the basement of another building. Creeping up the stairs, we find ourselves in an abandoned barn on the outskirts of the property. Clear tire marks can be seen and are fresh.

For the love of God, fuck!! Losing my shit a little, I kick a bucket close to me, sending it flying across the barn.

"He knew we were here and made an escape," Tank groans with frustration in his voice.

Fuck we were in the right place, but too late; or something or someone tipped him off we were here. Feeling dejected, we make our way back to the others.

"Tunnel leads to a barn on the edge of the property, fresh tire marks too. He knew we were here or were coming," Tank informs the others.

Everyone is feeling it as we trudge back to the vans and drive back to the clubhouse in silence. I can't believe he's one step ahead of us every goddamn time. How does he know?

Getting back to the compound, I need some time on my own. I head for the back of the compound and through the trail, which is barely noticeable between the trees. I walk along the trail for a while until I come to the clearing at the lake. Carrie and I used to love hanging here as kids, messing around in the water. I feel close to her here.

Sitting on the ground with my back against a tree base, I rest my head with my eyes closed. Taking deep breaths, I take a few minutes to sort my emotions out, which are running wild at the moment. I honestly don't know how to feel anymore. We're so close to finding her, and yet so far away too. I just want to find her and make sure she's okay. Especially after watching those videos. My hands fist at my sides as the pain and anger at seeing Carrie like that runs through my veins. Opening my eyes, I watch the moon reflect on the lake.

"Knew you'd be here," Tank says as he drops down beside me and rests against the tree.

"Remember all the fun we used to have out here as kids?"

"Fuck yeah, had my first time out here," I reply.

"No way! Who with?" says Tank.

"I don't kiss and tell."

"What happened to having no secrets?" scoffed Tank.

"Everyone has secrets," I declare.

At that bombshell, we sit in silence, watching the ripples on the lake. Both of us deep in thought and processing what happened tonight. Smacking Tank on the knee, I start to get up.

"Come on, brother, my ass is going numb, and I need to get back to my boy."

"Yeah, we need to bring Beau out here," says Tank.

"Good idea, we can make an afternoon of it. Food and get some inflatables for him."

"Need to teach him to swim," reminds Tank.

We walk back to the clubhouse in silence and head to our own rooms. After a quick shower, I slip into some board shorts and check on Beau. He's sleeping soundly.

I lean against the door jam and watch him sleep for a while. He looks so peaceful and like any normal kid. I need to find a psychologist for him to work on getting him ready for school and teaching him how to deal with what life has thrown at him in his short life already.

Leaving the door slightly open, I climb into bed and let my body relax into the mattress. This only makes my mind drift back to the mattress I saw in that room. It churns my guts to think Carrie and my boy had slept on that piece of shit for fuck knows how many years. With those images, I drift off to sleep.

With the sound of giggling and something tickling my nose, I open my eyes and find Beau on the bed next to me.

"Oh, so that's how it's going to be, huh?" I ask as I reach for him.

He moves out of the way and starts to jump on the bed. Leaning up, I snag him around the waist and pull him to me, tickling him as we fall onto the bed. His giggle is the most beautiful sound. Sitting us on the edge of the bed, I ask, "Breakfast, you little monkey?"

"I'm starving" is always the answer he replies whenever food is mentioned.

"Hop on," I reply.

I use my legs to make sure we don't fall off the bed with the force of him throwing himself onto my back.

I piggyback him into the kitchen with him laughing all the way. I set him down on the side while I get his breakfast ready. The guys start to filter in, all stopping to ruffle his hair or tickle him a little. He loves the attention, and I love that the guys aren't annoyed by him. It's not like we're used to kids running around.

After breakfast, I decide to spend a little time with him while we wait for Wire to find new leads. I know he's working as hard as he can to find Carrie.

CHAPTER ELEVEN

CARRIE

I'm curled up in the chair by the window watching the darkness of the woods that surround the house. Squinting to look a little closer, I'm sure I had seen movement. Watching the area more closely, I can't see anything else. It was probably a deer or some other animal. Relaxing back in the chair, I let my head fall against the armrest and close my eyes for a moment.

With that, my bedroom door flies open, and he comes running in.

"Grab a bag now," he demands.

He's frantic, throwing the bag at me.

"PACK!" he shouts.

Jumping to my feet, I quickly throw some clothes into the bag and also the last of the items that mean anything to me—a photo of my dad and me, a photo of Johnny, Jason, Scott, and me, and also the few baby items and photos Agnes was able to take of Beau and me.

Racing from the room, I meet him in the hallway. Grabbing my wrist, he pulls me down the hallway and the back stairs toward the basement. In the basement, he moves a wall that seems to lead down to a secret tunnel.

Just as he's closing the door, I can hear footsteps above me and shouts.

Everything gets still as we listen to them moving around upstairs. It is definitely more than one person from the footsteps. The basement door opens, which seems to knock him out of his trance. He quickly secures the hidden door, and we rush through the tunnel. He's pulling on my wrist, and I know it's going to leave a bruise.

We seem to be in the tunnel for ages before coming to another door leading into a barn. A car is sitting in the middle. He swings around quickly and grabs hold of my hair.

"Don't even try anything. You know what will happen if you do."

There is a threatening edge to his voice. Nodding, so he knows I understand, he throws our bags in the car.

"Get in and do everything I say."

I get into the passenger side of the car while he gets in the driver's side. We drive down an old track with the lights off until we hit the main road.

Turning onto the main road, he starts to drive, sticking to back roads.

"I'm guessing your boy has been reunited with his father."

My eyes widen. Agnes had found Jason, and he came for me. The thrill that runs through me has me feeling the smallest amount of hope. Hope I can get out of this and have something to go back to. I know getting away is not going to be easy, but I'm determined to make it back to my son.

We seem to be driving for hours, and my eyes start to drop.

"Sleep. It will be a few hours yet."

I do as I'm told. I lean my head against the window and watch the scenery go by, lulling me to sleep.

The slamming of a car door wakes me. Taking a moment to stretch and look around, we seem to be in the middle of the woods at some weird cabin.

My door opens, and he pulls me out. He's holding my other wrist so hard; I know I'll have matching bruises. Getting the bags, he pulls me behind him into the cabin. Looking around, it smells musty and has been empty for some time. Heading into the kitchen, he turns to me.

"Get this place cleaned up."

Not wanting to increase his mood any further, I head for the sink. Rinsing it out, I fill it with hot water and look under the sink for cleaning products and cloths. Finding some wash liquid and a few cloths, I get started on wiping down all the surfaces. I open a few windows to let some air in and wipe the glass down. I find a broom in a cupboard and sweep the whole downstairs. Finding a bucket in the same cupboard, I head upstairs and air out the bedroom and clean the bathroom.

By the time I'm finished, I'm covered in sweat and grime, but the place looks so much better.

I'm in the kitchen finishing the last of the cleaning when he comes back.

"You have done a good job, my pet. You will be rewarded."

He places his bag on the counter, and I notice a few guns on top. While he's outside at the car, I take a closer look and find a gun in the bottom, under the lining as if forgotten. Quickly taking the gun, I rush to the room I've claimed as mine and hide it. You never know when it may come in handy. Making my way back downstairs as if nothing is happening, I find him unloading a few groceries.

"You should be able to make something edible with this lot," he says.

Guess we're staying here for a while. Moving over to help, we quietly unpack the groceries.

"I have some business to attend to, my pet. You will be busy preparing our meal."

With that, he heads off down the hall. Deciding, for now, I'm going to play along, he needs to believe he has broken me even if it's just a little. The more he believes this, the more freedom he gives me. I busy myself making a quick pasta and tomato dish. Once this is ready, I make my way down the hall and knock on the office door.

"Come," he replies through the closed door.

Slowly pushing the door open, I say, "The food is ready."

Standing in the doorway, he watches me for a few moments.

"Thank you, pet. I'll be along in a moment." he replies.

Nodding my head, I close the door and head back to the kitchen. I plate up two meals and then sit at the table, waiting for him to join me. Once he's seated and starts to eat, he nods his head, and I start my food.

"My pet, we will have visitors this evening. Please ensure you're presentable and ready for when they arrive."

My stomach drops. No longer feeling hungry, I push my plate away.

Eyeing me from across the table, he states, "Eat up, my pet. You will need your strength."

Pulling the plate back toward me, I slowly start to eat again. I feel sick with every mouth full. He smiles and continues to finish his meal.

I honestly thought that with us being here, the abuse would stop. Wishful thinking, I guess. I really should have known better as this is not the first time he's moved us, and the abuse continued. He doesn't see it as abuse. The awful things he's done to me and the other girls, yes sadly over the years there have been others, really do turn him on. He thinks it's him showing us affection. Freud would say it is because he wasn't hugged enough as a child. Maybe that's true. Finishing as much of the meal as I can, I sit quietly and wait for him to finish.

"That was delicious, my pet. Now clean this up and get ready for our guests."

A violent shiver goes through me. Guests . . . as in more than one! That is never a good sign. Quickly cleaning the pots and wiping the kitchen down, I make my way to my room. Laid out on the bed are a matching bra and panties set, black with lace and a silk robe to wear over the top. Guess this is what he wishes me to wear.

The foreboding feeling in the pit of my stomach is telling me to run. With shaking hands, I clean up in the bathroom and then dress in the clothes provided. I slip on the pair of black heels he had also left. I sit on the edge of the bed and wait for him to come get me. I twist my hands together in my lap, all sorts running through my head. The bedroom door opens, and he appears.

"It is time, my pet."

Taking a deep breath, I get up from the bed and make my way toward him. Following him down the hall, thinking we're heading for the lounge area, but he stops and opens a door off the hall. The door leads to some stairs. Great a basement, nothing good happens in a basement. Following him down, I find the basement has been set up like his room at the house. His pleasure/torture tools are laid out to the side, and a massive bed-like bench is in the middle of the room. I can see several cameras set up around the room. There are also four men waiting, their faces covered in masks. Turning to face him, I see he's also now wearing a mask.

"This is a great honor I'm giving you. My pet is well trained. You all know the rules."

The men in the room nod. He guides me toward the bed and sits me on the edge.

"We shall begin," he starts.

He removes the remote from his pocket, and all the cameras come to life as he switches them on to record. Moving over to me, he strokes his hand along my cheek.

"My pet has been very well behaved and has greatly pleased me. She'll now be rewarded."

Pulling me to stand, he tugs on the cord holding the robe together, removing the robe from my shoulders. Turning me to face the other men, he trails his fingers over my collar bone and down between my breasts.

"Do you see what a tease you are, my pet? How much these men want you?"

Looking at the men, I can see the lust in their eyes. It is not a lust I want; this is a dark, evil glint. His hands are all over my body, causing my mind to go to its happy place. Any place is better than the here and now. He removes my bra and panties, forcing me to lie on the bed. He restrains my hands to each corner of the bed and the same with my legs, leaving me vulnerable and open. His hands continue to explore my body as he starts another demeaning sexual act.

Closing my eyes I continue to go to my happy place, wishing he would just hurry up. It seems to last forever before he's finished. Opening my eyes, I can see the other men are now naked.

"You have pleased me greatly, pet. You will now please my friends," he states.

He nods to the first man, who replaces him between my legs. Closing my eyes again, I block everything out as each man takes a turn.

After what feels like a lifetime, I become aware of what's around me. Blinking my eyes, I start to be aware of my surroundings. I'm still in the basement, and he's cleaning me up. I must have passed out from the pain at some point. He has a washcloth in his hand and is cleaning my body of blood.

"You're awake, my pet. You did so well and made me proud. I'll leave you to rest."

Once he's left the room, I take stock of my injuries. Nothing too bad, but my skin hurts on my thigh. Looking over, I can see small round burns on my hip and thigh. Great, they'd clearly burnt me with a cigarette. I'm covered in bruises, a few bite marks, and someone had also placed a few cuts on my arms.

Curling back up on the bed, I reach for the sheet and cover myself while I drift off to sleep.

I spend a few days down in the basement recovering. He brings me food and checks my wounds. After a few days, once he's happy I'm healing well, he informs me we will have guests this evening. He makes me dress the same as before, and once again, he leads four men into the basement. Not sure if these are the same men as before, but it is the same routine.

This continues for a while. I'm not sure how long I'm down in the basement, but I know it has to be a few weeks. Men come and abuse my body. He then cares for me while I heal, and we repeat the pattern.

It's now a few days since the last round. He comes into the basement.

"How are you feeling, my pet?" he asks.

Looking at him as if he's crazy. "I'm in pain."

I don't usually admit this, but my body needs a break. Scooping me up in his arms, he carries me upstairs to my room.

"Rest, my pet."

Glad he's gone, I make my way to the bathroom and into the shower. I just want to be clean. Scrubbing my body, but being careful around my burns and cuts. I stay in the shower for a while, letting the water run over me and wash away my tears as they stream down my face. Once the water is running cold, I get out and dry. Applying cream to my wounds, I curl back into bed and fall asleep as my body craves time to heal.

A week or two passes, and I'm able to get out of bed. Sitting at the kitchen table after making breakfast, he finally speaks.

"You have healed nicely, my pet. I'll give you a few more days before I have some very important guests. We will be having a party," he states.

My body shakes and I feel sick. No, just no! This is the worst it's ever been. I know I cannot take anymore. With the multiple men and the things they do to my body, I cannot survive anymore. My mind starts to spin.

"NO!" I scream as I jump out of my seat.

The look of shock and then rage on his face is almost comical.

"My pet, you do not get to decide. I own you, and you will do as you're told!" By the end, he's shouting at me. His face is red with rage.

"FUCK YOU!" I shout.

Yup, I've lost it. I know he wanted to break me, but not sure this is what he had in mind. The human body and mind can only cope with so much. I'm done!

"You're a sick, twisted, and evil person. I won't say man as you're not a real man. A real man doesn't need to abuse a woman to feel good about themselves. You're pathetic. You can't even get a woman, so you have to kidnap one. You have no clue how to treat a woman. As for giving me pleasure, that's a fucking joke. Your pencil dick couldn't cause pleasure if you tried. You need a map and a full guided tour to know how to please a woman," I rant.

Too caught up in my rant, I don't see his fist until it's too late. I start laughing hysterically.

"You even punch like a fucking little girl."

That was not the right thing to say and the final nail in my coffin as he launches himself at me, his hands wrap around my neck, and we're falling to the floor. We land with a thud, and his full weight is on top of me, his hands still wrapped around my neck. He starts to squeeze, and I can feel myself struggling to breathe. Remembering what my dad had told me about keeping calm and fighting back, I plant my feet firmly on the floor and using them as leverage, I buck my hips, trying to push him off. I claw at his face and try hitting him everywhere I can reach.

Managing to find his eyes, I push my thumbs into his eye sockets. The scream is ripped from him as he lets go of my neck, his hands going to his face. Rolling over and trying to get as much oxygen into my lungs, I attempt to stand up. I feel his hand in my hair as he grabs a handful and pulls me back to him.

"You stupid fucking whore!" he howls.

I kick back at him as he tries to smack my face into the cabinet, but not having the power after our fight earlier. Fuck, it still hurt as my face hit the wood.

"Get off me, you prick," I say. I keep kicking him, and he keeps punching me.

Feeling with my hands across the cabinet, I come across something cold. Wrapping my hand around the handle, I lift the frying pan and swing with all my might, colliding with his head. He seems dazed, and I manage to make my way down the hall to my room.

Running into the room, I slam the door closed and quickly find the gun I had hid earlier. My vision is starting to blur. I fumble, clicking the safety off, just as the door slams open, hitting the wall as he storms into the room. I point the gun in his direction.

"Don't come any fucking closer," I warn.

His laugh is maniacal.

"You don't have the guts to shoot me. You're weak and pathetic," he states. Smirking at me, he starts to step closer. "I broke you. You're MINE!"

Grinning back at him, I reply, "You never broke me and never will." With a maniacal laugh of my own, I add, "I hope you rot in hell!"

With my parting words, I empty the clip into him. I can see the shock on his face as he slumps to the floor. Dropping the gun, I feel my own body fall as the world goes black.

CHAPTER TWELVE

JOKER

I'm sitting in the family room with Beau as he decides what movie to watch next. Slowly we have been watching all the kids' movies I can think of, to try and work out what he likes without being too babyish for him.

"Well, well, never did I think I'd see the day big bad Joker would be watching a kids' movie," a feminine voice quips from behind me.

Turning to see the source of the voice, I see a blast from the past standing there.

"Kate?"

"In the flesh, baby," she replies.

Jumping off the couch, I pick her up in a hug and swing her around.

"When did you get back?" I ask her while completely shocked she's standing right in front of me.

Kate is Tank's sister and has been off dancing in New York. This girl is an amazing dancer.

"I got back earlier today. Who's the cute kid?" she asks.

Beau stops flicking through the channels and looks over at us.

"Come here, Beau. I want you to meet someone."

Coming over to us, he stands next to me.

"Beau, this is Kate. Kate, this is my son, Beau," I say as I put my hand on his shoulder.

The look of shock that flicks across her face is priceless.

"How long have I been gone?" she asks, laughing.

Holding out her hand to Beau, she says, "Well, it's nice to meet you, Beau."

Beau shakes her hand and then goes back to the television.

"Seriously, Joker, what the fuck have I missed?" she asks.

"Have you not seen Tank yet?" I reply.

"No, I came straight here from the airport. Wanted to surprise little bro," grinning as she says this.

"Oh, it will be a surprise for him," I state.

"Look, you know why I had to leave," she says, getting quiet.

I understand why she left, shit went down, and she felt she couldn't stay.

"He's still a member of this chapter," I remind her.

A soft look crosses her face.

"Can't hide forever. At some point, I have to pull my big girl pants up, flick him the bird, and get on with my life. It was his decision, not mine."

Yeah, Cass was completely in love with Kate, but shit went down, and he decided she couldn't handle the life. The thing is, she was raised in this life and knows nothing else. Cass, short for Cassanova, couldn't handle her being hurt, so he'd pushed her way. The only thing is, he had pushed too far and pushed her all the way to New York. At least she's home now.

"Anyway! Enough of the walk down memory lane. Where did Beau come from?" Kate asks.

"Beau is mine and Carrie's son," I explain.

Her face goes pale.

"Carrie is back? You found her?" she asks. You can hear the excitement in her voice.

"It's a long, complicated story," I reply. I take a breath, more for me than her. "Beau showed up with a woman who has been helping Carrie. She's being held by a sick psycho fuck. We have been searching for Carrie and got close a few times, but just missed them as he keeps moving them around. But Wire and some other whiz hacker are on the case. I'm getting my girl back!" I declare.

"Wow, Joker, that's a hell of a lot of information and a hell of a lot more you're leaving out too."

Kate always was too smart for her own good.

"Yeah, but I don't wanna put that crap in your head or talk about it with Beau so close."

Just then, the door opens, and in walks Tank.

"Brother, we got church," he states in an almost bored tone. He turns to leave until he gets a look at who I'm talking to. That stops him dead in his tracks and his eyes go wide with shock.

"Kate," he gasps.

"Miss me, little bro?" Kate asks.

Quicker than someone his size should be able to move, he scoops her up into his arms and gives her a massive hug.

"Fuck, when did you get back?" asks Tank.

"About 10 minutes ago. I came straight to the compound to look for you, but found Joker and Beau instead," she replies.

"Well, we have church, but you okay to wait for me? Then we can catch up."

"Yeah, I'll wait with Beau while you're all in church," she says.

Bringing her in for a hug of my own, I say, "Thanks, Kate. Beau, I got church, but Kate is going to stay with you."

Beau just nods his head and goes back to the television.

"Yeah, he's a little obsessed with that thing at the moment. He hasn't watched one before he came here, so we've been slowly introducing him to stuff," I declare sheepishly.

A concerned and confused look crosses her face.

"I'll explain later," I assure her.

She ushers us out and off to church. Leaving them in the family room, we join the rest of the brothers in church. Tank still has a huge smile on his face.

"What you smiling at?" Bull asks.

"Kate's back. She's in the family room with Beau," Tank confirms.

"Fuck brother, it will be good to have her ass back where it belongs," Bull replies. Bull has always thought of Kate as a daughter as she and Tank had spent so much time at our house when we were growing up.

I look over at Cass, his face is showing no emotion, but his eyes are showing everything he's feeling. That man still loves Kate.

"We going to have a problem?" Tank asks Cass.

"No," his short answer is very telling.

Tank just nods his head. Banging the gavel, BJ brings church to order.

"Okay, well, we will welcome Kate back later. As Bull said, it's good to have her home. Now back to our other Princess. Wire has found more videos. These are recent, and I've made the decision not to share them," he states.

Murmurs go around the room of why BJ had made this decision. Could they really be that bad?

"Why?" Reck asks before I can.

"Look, brother, I see how these videos affect you and Joker and the rest of the brothers too, for that matter. What good does it do for you all to see her like that? It won't help us find her, and we need everyone with a clear head," BJ demands.

This is why he's President. BJ is always a few steps ahead and see's everything from all angles.

"I wanna see them. I wanna know what is happening to my baby girl, so I know how best to help her. I don't want her to have to relive them by her having or feeling the need to tell us. That would break me more than seeing the videos," Reck declares.

"I feel the same as Reck. I don't wanna get her back and then do something that would trigger a flashback or upset her in any way," I add.

Prez seems to be thinking this through and looking to Bull. An unspoken conversation seems to be happening between them.

"Fine, Wire show them the latest video, but that's it," BJ states.

Wire nods and starts clicking away at his laptop. A few moments later, the screen in church comes to life.

"I warn you; this is not as bad as the others, but also worse at the same time."

Nodding, but not really understanding what he means until the video plays and I feel the vomit rise in my throat. He's right. It's not as bad as the others as they aren't assaulting her body as much. However, watching them doing a train on her is ripping my heart out. Each of them is taking turns to rape my girl. Some even burn her, and at times she tries to fight back. Turning to Reck, his head is in his hands.

"Turn it off," he cries.

"We did warn you, brother. This is the reason I didn't want to show you," Prez confirms.

"I get it, but we needed to know so we can help her," I say.

After a few moments of silence, while everyone gets a grip on what they just saw, Prez resumes church.

"We think we have a location of where the video was uploaded from. Now they are on the run. He's getting sloppy and slipping up. The location is a cabin in the woods a few miles out of town. We had thought of going in under the cover of darkness. However, most people who are on the run expect that, so we have decided to use the element of surprise and go early in the morning while they are sleeping."

I like this plan. The sooner we can reach her, the better.

"Get some sleep tonight and make sure all guns are clean and loaded. We ride first thing tomorrow morning." Banging the gavel to end church, Tank and I head straight for the family room.

Walking in, I find Beau bouncing around the couches.

"Dad, I'm Peter Pan, and Kate is Tinkerbell," he says as he flies from one couch to another.

Laughing, I turn to Kate. "I see you're corrupting my son with your Disney crap."

Kate is a huge Disney nut. She's always loved it, even when she was a kid. Seems she hasn't grown out of it.

"Dad, it was great. We watched Peter Pan and Mary Poppins. I'm going to tell Grandpops about the crocodile."

He runs off singing something about flying a kite in a fake British accent.

"Kid's a regular Dick Van Dyke," Kate laughs.

"Yeah, kid's got a great sense of humor. He does these impressions of the brothers. Cracks me up," Tank says.

"He's a good kid, Joker. He misses his mom," she adds.

With a sigh, I drop my head forward. I'd known this conversation was coming.

"Not now, sis! Just know we're going to a location tomorrow where we think Carrie might be," Tank says, giving his sister that look.

He may be the younger of the two, but he's always been protective. Not that Kate has ever really needed it. Kate is badass in her own right. When the shit went down with Cass, she didn't need saving as she saved herself. We just came in at the end and helped her clean up the mess. Tank and I made sure Kate could handle almost any weapon and is also mixed martial arts trained too. I smack Tank on the back.

"Thanks, brother. I'm going to make sure Beau hasn't managed to get into any trouble and leave you two to catch up. Kate, it's great seeing you, and I'm glad you're back. This is your home," I say. Giving her a big hug, she hugs me back.

"Thanks, Joker. It's good to be back and feels like home too."

Leaving them both to catch up, I head off to hunt my son down.

Later that night, once Beau is finally tucked in bed, I'm at the table in my room cleaning my guns. I know I need to be prepared for what's to come tomorrow. I still can't get the image of them sick fucks taking turns on my girl. When we get her back, we're going to have to make sure she's okay. Not sure how I'm going to bring it up, but she's going to need to be checked over by Doc to make sure there are no lasting effects on her, and also, who knows where they have stuck their cocks before. They could have passed anything onto Carrie, so we need to make sure she gets the medical help she needs. Once my guns are clean and all ready to go, I head downstairs to the bar. Maybe a shot or two would help me sleep. Just need something to switch off my thoughts.

Only a few brothers are at the bar, with Tank and Kate at a table in the corner. Cass is at the bar, his eyes on Kate.

"You okay brother," I ask.

"Yeah. Fuck Joker, I can't believe she's back."

"I know, been a long time," I reply.

"I thought over time, things would change. I did what I thought was right at the time. She was nearly hurt, because of me. It was my fault," he says with shame as he hangs his head.

Taking a swig from the beer that the prospect hands me, I level with him.

"Cass, that shit was not your fault. It was her crazy ex, not yours. You didn't do shit."

"Exactly, I didn't do shit to help her," he interrupts, raising his voice.

He storms out of the room, slamming the door on his way out. Looking over at the table, Kate is watching the closed door. Her eyes then find mine, and there is sadness in them. Their story is not over. Grabbing my beer, I head over to join them.

"Is he okay?" Kate asks as I sit down.

"Yeah."

"He's not happy I'm back." She seems sad by this like she wants him to be happy.

"He's just dealing with some shit, sweetheart. He'll come around. We're all thrilled as fuck you're back," I say as I put my arm around her shoulder.

She smiles at this and nudges my side.

"I missed everyone too. You boys need someone to keep you in check and bail you out," she laughs.

Faking like I'm hurt. "You wound me. I'm a saint."

Tank nearly chokes on his beer, spraying the liquid everywhere, some even coming out his nose.

"Fuck off, brother," he says between coughs.

Kate and I crack up, laughing so hard at the look on his face. God, I needed that laugh.

"Where's Beau?" Kate asks.

"He's asleep. Only took 3 stories this time," I chuckle, realizing just how much my life had changed over the last few weeks.

Pip had bought him a load of books. He can read, but not great. Every night, we have been reading at bedtime. He's coming along great.

"I need to sort out the paperwork for him, so we can get him into school," I remember.

"Speak to Prez. Maybe the club lawyer can help," says Tank.

Bloody good idea, and I make a note to speak to Prez after we get sorted tomorrow. My first job is getting his mom back for him.

"Right, I'm heading off. Need to be rested for tomorrow," I declare.

"I'll stay with Beau tomorrow. BJ has given me my own room here for as long as I need it. I'll get sorted and then find a place of my own. Not that you guys aren't great, but I don't wanna be living here full time. Want a place of my own," Kate says.

"Thanks, Kate," I say with a genuine smile on my face.

Tank doesn't look happy about Kate moving out of the compound. I know he only just got his sister back, but now that I have Beau, I understand where she's coming from. It's not exactly peaceful at the clubhouse. But on the other hand, it is safe.

I'd noticed a few days ago the land to the West of the clubhouse is for sale. It's a large chunk of land. I had the idea we could pull resources and buy the land to build houses on for the core members of the club first and then anyone else who wants one. This would ensure the families are protected, but also have space from the main clubhouse. I'd need to bring it up at church after we get Carrie back. I check on Beau. The boy is sleeping like a baby. Making my way to my own bed, I get settled and try to sleep. Hopefully, we would be bringing Carrie back with us tomorrow.

The next morning I'm one of the first up. After a quick shower, I re-check my guns, and I'm ready to go. The mood in the clubhouse is a mix of nervous energy and rage. We all meet in the main room.

"We stay together as planned, no one's to be hero, and we all come back. Watch each other's backs. Let's go!"

With Prez's orders, we all head to the vans. The bikes would be too loud and alert anyone to us coming. I'm in a van with Prez, Reck, Bull, Tank, Cass, and a few others. It takes about 30 minutes to get a few miles from the cabin. We pull off the road and hide the van in the forest. From here, we head to the cabin on foot. We settle at the edge of the forest and watch the cabin. All seems quiet, eerily quiet. It all feels off to me. My gut knows it.

Nudging Tank next to me, "Something's off, brother," I declare.

He nods his head and gets his phone out.

"Prez and Bull feel the same, so do a few others," he adds.

We wait a little longer, and no movement is seen inside.

"Okay, you, me, and Bull are taking the front, Prez, Reck, and Cass are taking the back. Everyone else surrounds the cabin in case we need them," Tank orders.

Nodding, we slowly make our way toward the cabin. The uneasy feeling grows as we get closer. We reach the front door, and just before Tank kicks it in, I grab him to stop. Pointing at the door, flecks of red can be seen. Tank lets the others know; we had found blood on the front door. Slowly Tank opens the door, and the smell of death hits us.

"Fuck, this is not good." It's out of my mouth before I can stop it.

There is blood everywhere, and there has definitely been a fight. The place is trashed. The others come from the back and confirm the kitchen is much the same. Heading down the hall, smudges of blood are everywhere as if someone was running. My heart drops, thinking this could be Carrie's blood, and we could be too late. The bathroom is clear and the other bedroom. Reck opens the door that seems to lead to the basement. He heads down with Bull behind him. Tank and I carry on down the hall toward the remaining bedroom. The smell of death is getting stronger. Pushing the door open, a man's body is slumped in the corner. Blood is everywhere, pooling around the man. Clearly, he's the smell of death. Prez joins us in the bedroom.

"This is the guy from the video," he states.

My head turns to Prez. "How do you know? We never saw his face."

Turning to face me, I can tell by his face he doesn't want to tell me.

"There was one other video that we didn't share with anyone. He showed his face in it," Prez explains.

"You kept another video from us?" I rage. My hands are fisted at my sides, and I'm shaking. Tank places his hand on my shoulder. Not sure if it's to calm me, hold me back, or because he's feeling the same level of rage as me.

"This video was different from all the others. It was more like couple porn. You could tell she wasn't willing, but it was softer," he confirms. "You didn't need that shit in your head. From the video, you would think he loved her. So yes, I kept it from you," Prez adds warily.

I start to settle a little. He's right, that shit would have fucked with me more, but I'm still pissed. Storming from the room, I meet everyone else outside.

"She's not here. The sick fuck that had her is dead in the bedroom."

"Could she be elsewhere?" one of the other guys calls out.

Just as I start to think about that question, Tank and Prez come running from the cabin.

"Get to the vans quick," shouts Prez.

We all take off running, fuck what's going down now!

CHAPTER THIRTEEN

CARRIE

Slowly I start to come back around. My head is pounding, and my body hurts all over. Shaking, I attempt to sit up. The pain is worse now that I'm sitting up straight. Taking a look around, I'm still in the cabin. He's slumped in the corner, blood pooling around him. You can smell death in the air. Fuck I had killed a man. I know it was either him or me, but I still took a life.

I'm shaking as I try to stand, holding onto the dresser for support. I need to get out of here before one of his, *'guests,'* come. Who knows what would happen if they got a hold of me? Grabbing my bag from under the bed, I pull out some clothes and my personal bits I can't live without, throwing them into the bag. In the bathroom, I grab some medical supplies and anything else I may need. I have no clue where I am, but I know where I'm going. I'm going home.

After grabbing what I can, I find the car keys and head outside. The car is parked at the side of the cabin. Throwing my bag on the seat next to me, I get in and drive down the hill toward the road. Once I'm at the end of the drive, I need to decide which way to turn, left or right. After sitting there for a few moments trying to decide, I follow my gut and turn left. I keep driving until I pass through a small town and out onto the main highway. I've not been driving for too long when I see a sign that makes my entire body tingle with happiness. Home!

I was closer than I knew. Heading in the direction the sign says, I follow the road until it all starts to look familiar. My head is feeling woozy again, so I put my foot down and head for the compound, praying it is still in the same place. Just as I come around the bend, the gates are up ahead, all lit up, guiding me home. I'm getting dizzy and know I'm going to pass out again soon. I put my foot down more and head straight for the gates, passing out just before I crash through them.

I wake up as I'm being carried. Looking up, I see a face I would never forget.

"Wolf," I gasp.

"Oh, thank fuck. I got you, girly." I can sense the worried tone in his voice.

Curling up further in his arms, I'm finally feel safe. I had made it. I'm home. With that thought, I pass out again.

I wake again, and this time I'm lying on something soft. I don't seem to be able to move anything, and the pain is unreal. I can hear voices.

"Doc, why isn't she waking up?"

"Calm down, son. She's been through hell, and her body needs time to heal. Also, her mind will too. She'll wake up when she's ready."

I know those voices. It's Jason and Doc. I want to tell them I'm awake, I'm here, but my stupid body won't listen. The blackness starts to claim me again.

"Please, babydoll, just open those pretty blue eyes for me. I need you, baby. Beau needs you. Please come back to us."

Jason's voice wakes me. He's gripping my hand, and I feel wetness on my hand. Is he crying? I want to go to him. I want to see his smile again. Why won't my stupid body do as it's told? The blackness once again claims me.

Another voice wakes me this time, and it's a voice I've missed for so long.

"Angel, I'm so sorry. I've been a useless father. I should have never left you. I thought your mother would have cared for you. I'm so sorry I left you with her. Johnny is here too. Please wake up so we can all be together. I've met my grandson. He's a right little comedian. He's amazing, angel. You've done so well with him. I'm proud of you, angel. Please, please come back to me."

Daddy? He's here? It makes my heart soar that he's met Beau and loves him. I really want to wake up. I want to be with my family, but it hurts too much.

"Carrie, I need you to wake up. Joker, he's not doing so well. We've lost you once, and we don't want to lose you again. He won't survive losing you twice. He never stopped looking for you. None of us did."

Scott, he's mine and Jason's best friend. But who is Joker?

"Please, Carrie. I need my best girl back. Joker and me . . . Crap, sorry. Jason. We patched into the club. Jason's road name is Joker and mines Tank. I'm not a scrawny little boy anymore, Carrie. Please come back to us."

I'm so happy they both got their wish and patched into the club. It was all they had talked about growing up. How they were going to be just like Bull, BJ, and my dad. They deserve to be part of the club. I wonder if it's changed much since I was last here. That is my last thought as the blackness comes again.

"Sis, can you hear me? You need to wake up as everyone is freaking the fuck out. I know you're strong, and you'll come back to us when you're ready. I just wanted to thank you for everything you did for me, to protect me. I wouldn't be the man I am today without you. You truly are the greatest sister. I love you. Rest and come back to us when you're ready."

A tear slowly falls down my cheek. Johnny!

Waking, I feel a whole lot better. The pain isn't so bad. I can feel a little hand in mine and a soft kiss on my hand.

"Momma, I miss you. Daddy says you're feeling poorly and need sleep to feel better. I'm glad Daddy is looking after you. I miss you, Momma. I want to show you my awesome room and the bike that Grandpa Reck bought me that matches Daddy's. I even have my own cut as BJ, he's the Prez, said I'm part of the club."

Beau! That voice is music to my ears. He sounds so confident and strong. Clearly, being at the club was the best thing for him. I tried to move my hand and managed to move my fingers a little.

"DADDY," Beau screams, thundering boots sound around the room.

"Beau, what's the matter?" Jason asks hurriedly.

"Momma moved her fingers," he declares.

The second he finishes his sentence, his hand is replaced in mine by a large, rougher hand.

"Babydoll, can you hear me? Squeeze my hand if you can hear me."

I can hear the desperation in his voice. I try with all my strength to squeeze his hand. I hear the sharp intake of breath when I manage it.

"Get Doc, she squeezed my hand."

Opening my eyes, I'm greeted by Jason's handsome face leaning over me.

"Jason," I croak. God, my throat is sore.

"Fuck, Babydoll, you scared the shit out of us," he puffs out with a nervous laugh as he swipes his hand across the top of his head.

Jason has tears running down his face. Beau is dancing next to him, singing something about me being awake.

"Don't swear in front of Beau," I chastise him

"Awake two seconds and you're already busting my balls." He smiles as he says this causing me to smile too.

At that moment, my dad, Scott, Johnny, and Doc burst into the room.

"Hi, guys," I croak.

Dad rushes to my bedside and grabs my hand, tears running down his face. Scott moves closer to Jason, placing his hand on his shoulder as a gesture of support. Johnny stays near the door, seeming unsure of where his place is.

Reaching out my other hand toward Johnny, I say, "Johnny, come here." He takes a moment and slowly shakes his head.

"Kid, she's okay," Jason confirms.

Beau walks over to his uncle and tugs on his sleeve. Johnny looks down at him while Beau slowly takes his hand and pulls him over to the other side of my bed.

"It's okay, Uncle Johnny, Momma's a badass," Beau declares.

The silence in the room is broken when we all burst out laughing. God! My kid rocks! I can't even be mad at him for his language. Johnny sits on the side of the bed, and I reach for him.

"I see you grew up good."

A huge smile stretches across his face.

"I missed you, sis," he says as a lone tear escapes from his left eye.

"Missed you too, kid," I reply as I quickly wipe it away.

Looking at the cut he's wearing, I start to smile.

"Guess the apple doesn't fall far from the tree."

Everyone laughs.

"Yeah, the brothers found me and took me in. I've been living here at the compound since then," Johnny confirms.

I'm really glad Johnny had the guys to help him while I couldn't. At least he had a loving family.

"Angel, what can you tell us? What do you remember?" my dad asks, using my old nickname he had called me when I was little.

I know Dad and probably the rest of the guys want to know what happened and where I have been all this time. I vaguely remember hearing bits of conversations while I was asleep.

"Come now, brother, plenty of time for all that. Why don't you all go tell everyone the good news while I check the patient over," Doc orders.

With kisses and hugs, they all leave, except Jason. I knew he wouldn't be going far. Doc checks me over. I hiss a little when he checks my ribs, causing Jason to leap out of his chair and race to my side.

"Fuck Doc, she's hurt enough," he exclaims.

Giving him a side-eye, Doc continues his examination.

"Sorry, son, but I'm going as gently as I can. Need to check if any are broken. The good news looks like they're just badly bruised. You're going to be sore for a while," confirms Doc.

He's looking like he wants to say more, but is debating saying it.

"Just ask what you need to Doc," I say, placing my hand on his arm

"I hate to ask this, but I need to run an internal exam. I'm sorry, Carrie. I really do hate to say this."

You can see the pain written across his face. Looking over at Jason, pain and anger are also showing on his face. Fuck, this can only mean one thing.

"You've seen the videos, haven't you?" I confirm.

A look of guilt flashes across both their faces that tell me I'm right. Fuck I didn't want anyone to ever see them. I knew they would be shown somewhere as otherwise why would he film us to start with. But God, I was praying it was for his own sick pleasure.

"Who else has seen them? Has everyone seen them?" I'm starting to panic now. I try to sit up, but Doc stops me. "No, Doc, tell me!" I cry out.

I'm shouting now and getting more upset, but I don't seem to be able to calm down. I can feel the tears on my cheeks. This can't be happening. From the look on their faces, I know everyone has seen them. Well, at least all the brothers. I can't handle this.

"Get out. GET OUT!" I scream.

I turn over so my back is to them and pull the covers up to my chin so I'm fully covered.

"Carrie," Jason starts to say with his hand on my shoulder.

I move so he can't touch me, "Don't touch me. Just leave me alone," I beg.

"Come on, son, let's give her a moment," says Doc in a defeated tone.

A few moments later, I hear the door open and then close. Once it's closed, the dam breaks, and I sob into my pillow. Fuck, they all know what had happened to me. Do they think less of me? Are they disgusted at the sight of me?

I cry until I can't cry anymore, too exhausted to do anything, but fall asleep.

I wake the next morning feeling like I've got a hangover from all the crying. A fresh bottle of water and some Advil are on the bedside table. Taking the tablets and a drink of water, I slowly make my way to the bathroom to take care of business.

Back in bed, I know I need a plan. I don't want to stay here with them all looking at me with pity or disgust. I'm not sure which is worse.

I need to heal, find a job and a house for Beau and me. I need to reclaim my life. I had honestly never thought about what would happen or how I would feel if someone saw those videos. The things I had done to me in my most vulnerable moments. I'm stronger than that. Those videos shouldn't define me, but I know looking at the brothers' faces, I know they saw it all. A knock at the door brings me out of my head. Doc enters with a woman.

"Carrie, it's good to see you awake," says Doc with caution.

He comes closer and the woman follows him.

"This is Dr. Whitelaw, I know I mentioned an internal examination yesterday, but I felt you might be more comfortable with a female doctor," he explains.

Poor Doc, he was only trying to help me, and I'd lost my shit with him. Giving him a small smile, I nod my head.

"Thank you, Harry. Hi Carrie, my name is Helen. Are you okay with me doing your examination today, or

I can come back when you're feeling more up to it?" she asks, giving me a warm smile. A very motherly feeling radiates off the doctor.

"No, now is fine. I just want this over with."

Doc nods his agreement. "I'll leave you ladies. Just shout if you need anything."

He then quietly leaves the room. Sitting on the edge of the bed, Dr. Helen explains what's going to happen.

"I understand you have been through something traumatic. If at any point you feel uncomfortable, please just say so, and we will stop. I want to give you this card, it's for a psychologist. She's wonderful and has a lot of experience with helping people in your circumstances."

Looking down at the purple card that reads Tracy Wood, a healing hand. I'll definitely consider calling her.

Dr. Helen continues to explain what tests she'd run and the exam she's going to need to do. Nodding my head that I understand, she moves the sheet to uncover my legs and helps me remove my underwear. Feeling vulnerable at being so open, she gives me a soft smile.

"I'll be as quick as I can for you, remember if it gets to be too much, just let me know, and we can stop."

Nodding, I let her know I understand.

"I just want this over with, please," I beg.

Giving me another of her soft smiles, she does exactly what she said she would, and it's over quicker than I thought it would be.

"I'll let you know as soon as I have the results for you. Do you have any questions?"

Feeling a little nervous to ask, but I need to know.

"Am I okay . . . down there? Does anything look like it shouldn't?"

God, I sound pathetic.

"You're fine Carrie, everything is as it should be," she reassures.

At her words, I release the breath I didn't realize I was holding.

"Thank you," I say as the tears start to come again.

"You're welcome, Carrie, now you get some more rest and call me anytime," Dr. Helen says.

Leaving me with her card and my thoughts, Dr. Helen quietly leaves the room.

Turning over, I stare at the wall. Feeling a little dirty, I make sure the bedroom door is locked and head for the shower.

Painfully undressing while the water warms up, I check that the towel on the rail is clean and walk under the hot spray. I let the water run over me and wash all my thoughts away. Grabbing the body wash, it smells woody and manly, but at this point, I'm past caring. Once I'm washed clean, I stay under the water, letting the warm feeling seep into my bones, making me human again. Once the water starts to run cold, I get out. Wrapped in the towel, I go on a hunt for some clothes. Finding only men's clothes, I steal a t-shirt and a pair of boxers.

Sitting back on the bed, I'm not sure what to do next.

Hearing laughter from outside, I go to the window. A massive playset has been set up, and Beau is running riot around it, with a couple of the brothers chasing and playing with him. His laugh and smile warming my heart. Tearing up again, I give myself a mental slap. I need to pull myself together. I can't keep crying all the time. But seeing Beau so free and happy is a miracle. Clearly, being here with his dad has been the right thing. Watching Jason join Beau in the mini playground, He's such a good Dad. My heart hurts from all the time they had missed out on. Jason looks up and sees me watching.

I move away from the window, checking the door is still locked. I crawl back into bed. I'm not ready to face them.

CHAPTER FOURTEEN

JOKER

Seeing Carrie standing at the window watching us with tears falling down her face is too much. I tell Beau I'll be back in a minute, and I make my way back inside to my room, where Carrie is staying. Standing outside the door, I'm not sure whether to knock or just walk in. The way she reacted when she realized we had all seen the videos was heartbreaking. She was so upset. I just wanted to comfort her, but that seemed to be doing more damage. Hanging my head forward, I lean it against the door.

Looking down, I notice a pair of boots come into view.

"Give her time, son. She'll work it all out."

I knew Doc wouldn't be far from her.

"She needs to be checked out, Doc. We need to help her," I say as my voice cracks. I had finally got her back, but I feel like I'm losing her again.

"Already had a female doctor friend of mine visit her. It's all been taken care of, son," replies Doc.

Looking up at him, he has a sad smile.

"Is she okay?" I stammer out. Fuck I couldn't cope if anything is wrong with her.

"Said everything looked good, and she should have the test results as soon as possible."

Okay, so a few days and we would know what we're dealing with, if anything. Okay, so just need to keep busy. Stop my mind from wandering and no googling stuff, or I'd be a nervous wreck in the corner thinking she has all sorts of things.

"Get out of your head Joker. She'll be fine." Jesus, where did Wolf come from? For a big fella, he sure moves silently.

"Thanks, Wolf," I say.

"Damn near gave me a heart attack when she plowed her car through the gate, and I realized it was her. Fuck, I couldn't get to her quick enough," said Wolf.

Looking confused, smashed gate?

Chuckling, he pats me on the back.

"Your girl came crashing through the gate with her car while you were off looking for her. We'll go over everything in church later. The main concern was checking she was okay and getting the medical attention she needed," he explains, making things a little clearer.

Letting out a breath, I know I'm going to be pissed, but proud when I hear the full story.

"Come on, son, give her some time," Doc says gently.

Pulling me away from her door, I head downstairs and back outside to play with Beau for a while before church. Kate comes out and joins in the fun.

A little while later, a prospect comes out to tell us it's time for church.

"I'll stay and play some more," Kate says before I've even had a chance to say anything.

"Thanks, Kate," I say, thankful for all her help.

Leaving Kate playing Peter Pan with Beau, I make a note to build him a treehouse like the one from the movie.

I head into church, seems I'm the last one in again.

"Alright boys, settle down. We're all happy to have not only Carrie back with us, but also Kate. It seems like our Princesses are all finding their way home."

There are a lot of cheers, hoots, and hollers from the brothers. Everyone is happy they are both back home safe.

"Carrie made a grand entrance. Seems she put up a fight and managed to drive from the cabin to the clubhouse. She passed out just before reaching the gates, causing her car to plow through them. I've got the prospects fixing the gate, but this gives us an excuse for a new, more secure gate. Sarg, I need you on that as our security expert. Maybe review all our security and see where improvements can be made," orders Prez.

Sarg nods his head, he's been mentioning updating our security for a while.

"I haven't managed to speak with Carrie as I'm giving her time to heal and get used to being back before I ask her the hard questions. That isn't going to be easy for any of us. I've spoken with Doc, and it seems Carrie figured it out that we have all seen the videos. She's not happy about it and reacted badly. Locked herself in her room for now and will only see Beau.

Let's give her time. It is a lot for one person to handle. Doc has arranged for a female doctor he knows to see her. Hopefully, that will make her feel more comfortable," continues Prez.

Doc nods and fills us in a little more.

"Helen Whitelaw is a trusted colleague and friend. She's already seen Carrie and is running tests to check all is okay. We should have the results within the next few days as she's put a rush on it. She's also given Carrie a card from a psychiatrist named Tracy Wood, who is a specialist in these kinds of situations. Hopefully, Carrie will feel up to speaking with her so she can start to deal with what has happened to her and move forward."

Wow, they really have been looking after my girl for me. It's killing me that she won't see me. The devastation I saw in her eyes when she realized we had seen the videos broke me. I never want her to look at me like that again.

"Thanks, Doc, keep us informed. Any other business?" asks Prez.

Now seems like a good time to raise my idea.

"I had an idea, Prez," I say.

"Okay, son, the table is yours," Prez replies.

"I've been thinking about our living situations. I have Beau now and want to spend as much time as possible with him. But I know I'm needed at the clubhouse. I had the idea of building our own street within the compound. We could build a few houses to start for brothers with families and then expand for single brothers or anyone who wants one. We can also keep a few for visitors. Kate could even have one so that way she would have her own space to come and go as she pleases, but she would be safe within the compound."

A few brothers murmur from around the table about it being a good idea, helps me relax. I really hope they go for it.

"I like the idea. We would need to check finances and work out costs, but saying that, we don't have much room left in the compound," Prez says.

"I've thought of that. The large plot of land to the West of the compound has just gone up for sale. We buy that and expand the compound. That land is massive, and the price is low, so it would be a steal," I add.

Prez smirks at me before shaking his head.

"You've thought of everything, son," he says with pride in his voice. "Okay, get us prices, costs, time scale, and also a rough plan. If it seems viable, we'll vote and get started," Prez adds, putting an end to the meeting.

The thought of getting my teeth stuck into this project makes me swell with pride. I already can see what it should look like in my head. The board having a street to themselves, then trusted brothers another street, and visitor houses another. It would be like our own little town.

Leaving church, I head for Carrie's room. I know the brothers had said to give her time, but I want her to know I'm here. Kate took Beau out for the day. That girl loves my son and is taking her aunt duties seriously.

Getting to Carrie's door, I knock. Hearing no sounds and getting no answers, I knock again. No reply, but I know she's in there. Sliding down the wall, I plant my arse on the floor.

"Carrie, it's me, baby. I know you can hear me. I just want to check how you're doing." I say hesitantly.

Deciding now is probably a good time to let her know how I'm feeling. I stay sitting next to the door and just keep talking.

"I've missed you, baby. I never stopped looking for you. None of us did. I'm so sorry we couldn't find you sooner. I wish I could have stopped all you have been through. But I'm proud as fuck too. Carrie, you managed to raise the most amazing son. He's perfect. The brothers love him. He's so funny. Did I tell you Kate is back? Yeah, she turned up a week or so ago. Beau loves her. She's got him today; they've gone on an aunt adventure, she called it, so fuck only knows what trouble they will get into." I can't help a little chuckle coming out as I tell her that.

"I made sure to send two prospects with them just in case. He's safe, baby, but we both know the mischief she can get into. The pair of you together was a nightmare. Always getting into stuff you shouldn't be. You were partners in crime."

The memories of Carrie and Kate together make me chuckle. If there was trouble to be found, those two would find it.

"There hasn't been a day that I haven't thought about you or shared stories with Johnny and Tank. Having Johnny here helped, but we missed you. God, how we have missed you! I understand you need time, but I need you to know that I'm here. You're my girl."

I'm starting to waffle now, and I get the feeling she isn't going to talk, so I move to get up and make my way down the hall. A small voice stops me dead.

"Jason."

Slowly turning, I see Carrie standing just outside the door in one of my t-shirts. Fuck she looks good in my clothes. Time seems to slow down as we stand just staring at each other. Making my way to her, she stays standing in the doorway.

"Wanna go inside?" I say.

Not wanting to come across as pushy, but she seems to be only wearing my t-shirt, and I don't want anyone else to see her like that. Nodding, she goes back into the room and gets under the sheet. Sitting on the edge of the bed, I make sure to give her room.

"How are you feeling? Are you still in pain?" I start to reel off the questions.

"I'm feeling better. The pain isn't too bad. Not the worst I've felt, so manageable," she replies quietly.

I flinch at that statement, I honestly tried not to, but fuck, she should never feel pain. Looking at her, she looks sad. Before I realize what I'm doing, more questions follow.

"Do you need anything? Clothes, women stuff?" I ask nervously.

"Women stuff?" she chuckles

"Yeah, you know, nice smelling girly shit," I shrug.

This makes her laugh, and fuck if it is not the best sound ever. It makes me smile, and I want to keep hearing that for the rest of my life.

"Yeah, dude, I get whatcha mean. Girly shit and some clothes would be nice," she says, still giggling. "Whose room is this?" she asks.

"Oh, this is my room," I confirm.

"Ah, well, I'm wearing your boxers and shirt, sorry," she replies sheepishly.

Fuck, the thought of her in my boxers has my cock standing to attention. Not now, man! Getting my phone out, I text Kate, she replies, saying she and Beau will sort it while they are out.

"Kate is going to get you some stuff while she's out with Beau," I tell her.

"Thank you, Jason," she says, giving me a slight smile.

"You're welcome. Anything you need, just let me know," I say as I can't stop looking at her.

I can see her looking at my cut. She runs her fingers over the patch showing my road name.

"Now that road name has got to have a story," she teases.

Laughing, she has no idea.

"You remember I've always been a bit of a joker, pulling pranks and stuff?" I ask as she nods her head in agreement. "When I was a prospect, we went to a traveling fair. There was this Joker dancing around. The idiot lost his footing and fell, taking me with him. He ended up on top of me. The guys thought it was hilarious and said I'd been *'jokered.'* I got called Joker ever since," I end with a shrug.

By the time I'm finished, Carrie is holding her stomach, laughing so much. The sight is amazing; she looks so free and happy.

"That is the best story ever," she says between giggles.

"Glad I can amuse you," I say with my own chuckle.

Gracing me with a soft smile, she innocently tucks a strand of hair behind her ear, causing my cock to wake up again. Damn it!

"How has Beau been?" she asks.

Knowing how important our son is to her makes me want her more.

"He's been great. He's really coming into himself. Prez has helped me get a lawyer so we can make sure he has the right paperwork, so he can start school," I rush out, my voice laced with excitement.

Her face drops, and I know I've said the wrong thing.

"I'm so sorry, Jason," she says as she puts her head in her hands.

Unable to stop myself, I reach for her and cradle her against me.

"Babydoll, you did the best job you could with the situation you were in. You have nothing to be sorry about. He's a great kid. He's so clever. You taught him well," I reassure her.

Holding her tightly against me, but not too tightly that I hurt her, I run my hands down her hair in a soothing motion. I just want to comfort her and make sure she knows we're in this together. I repeat those words out loud for Carrie to hear.

"We're in this together now, Carrie. I'm his dad, and I'm going to step up to help."

Raising her head, she gives me a small smile, cupping my face.

"You're a good man, Jason Davis."

Looking into her eyes, I can see the mix of emotions she's feeling. The moment is broken when Beau comes bounding into the room.

"Momma, Dad, I've had the most amazing day with Aunt Kate," he shouts as he dives onto the bed and crawls between us.

"That's great, kid," I say, ruffling his hair.

He swats my hand away, which causes us all to laugh. Kate comes in the room, weighed down with bags, a prospect following behind with more bags and a scowl on his face. Dumping the bags on the floor, he leaves muttering about stubborn women, pains in his ass as he leaves. Guess Kate has not behaved herself.

"Hey girlie, got you all the shit you need," Kate says as she dumps her bags.

"Yeah, Momma, I helped pick out some girly shit," Beau confirms with a big grin on his face.

Coughing to hide my laugh, he looks so freaking cute and proud of himself.

"Thanks, baby, but don't copy the naughty words you hear." Carrie tries to tell Beau off, but is struggling to keep her laugh in.

"Okay, Momma, I'm off to play."

With that, he's off again at speed. Jesus, how much energy does the kid have? The three of us look at each other and burst out laughing.

"Okay, I'll grab some clothes and sort some space out for you to put all this away. I'll stay in one of the other rooms," I tell her.

Carrie starts to protest, but I shut her down.

"Babydoll, this room adjoins to Beau's. It makes more sense for you to stay in here, so you're close to him. I'll move across the hall so I can still hear if you or he needs anything," I reassure her.

Smiling, I set about moving some of my stuff into the room across the way so Carrie can have some space for all her new stuff. Once I'm sorted, I leave the girls to it and head down to the bar for a drink and to check on Beau. I love my son, but he's definitely my son and gets into all sorts of trouble without trying. Finding him in the main room, he's sitting with Reck and Tank.

"Beau is telling us about his good job for the day," Reck says as he and Tank are laughing. Guess the kid said girly shit again. Shaking my head, I join them.

"You using bad language again, kid?" I ask, trying to use my best Dad voice. This only seems to cause Reck and Tank to crack up more.

"Just saying how it is, Dad," he says as he runs off outside.

Jesus, that kid is going to be a handful.

"Same as you were at his age, gobby little shit." Bull joins in laughing.

"Guess it's karma for the crap I pulled on you then." I laugh at the smirk on his face.

"You weren't too bad, a good kid, really. Just too much like your Pops," Pip says as she joins us laughing too.

"Thanks, Pip. At least someone still loves me."

Laughing, she kisses the top of my head. Pip has always been a mother figure and still is to all that enter the clubhouse. We're a family, and that's what counts.

"How's Carrie doing?" Pip asks.

"Yeah, she's doing okay. We talked a little earlier. She's with Kate now. I got her clothes and girly shit to try and make her feel better," I reply.

"I'm sure it will help. Glad the both of you are talking. I might just pop up and check on the girls. You know the trouble those two can get into without trying."

She laughs as she walks off down the hall. She really isn't wrong.

CHAPTER FIFTEEN

CARRIE

It's been a month now since I escaped, and I'm healing. My bruises have gone, ribs have nearly fully healed, and I'm starting to feel more like my old self. After about a week or so when I could move better, I made an appointment with Tracy Wood, the psychiatrist Dr. Whitelaw had recommended. She's really nice and welcoming. Talking to her is really helping.

I have a session once a week. Joker drives me, waits for me to be done, and then takes me to do something nice to cheer me up. Some of the sessions are hard, and I'm physically and mentally exhausted some days. But I know getting it all out is good for me. I'm starting to realize this was not my fault. I didn't cause these things to happen to me. I'm also not a victim, but a survivor, which shows my strength. I still have a very long road to go before I'm completely coping, but that would all come in time. I'd never forget what happened to me, but with Tracy's help, I'm learning to live with it all, and she's giving me the tools to reclaim my life.

Joker has been amazing and so patient with me. I don't know when or if I'll ever be ready to be with a man again. I need to be able to stand on my own two feet and provide for Beau and me. Joker has said I don't need to worry about it, but I need this for me. I don't want to be swallowed whole again by a man, to become reliant on him or anyone.

To make this step forward, I need to move Beau and me out of the clubhouse. We need a place of our own. A home my son deserves. I would never stop Joker from seeing Beau. Women who use their children as weapons against their dads make me sick. You're only punishing the children more, and every child needs their dad in their life. I go to find my dad. I find him in the garage.

"Hey Dad, you got a moment?" I ask.

He looks up from the truck he's working on.

"For you, anything," he replies.

Smiling, he follows me outside, and we take a seat on the picnic table away from everything so we can talk.

"How's the therapy going?" he asks.

Dad has been great in my recovery, making sure I have everything I need and ensuring I know he loves me.

"It's going good, Dad. That's what I want to talk to you about," I reply.

"Okay, petal, what's up?"

"I'm so grateful you've allowed me to stay here while I'm healing. But now my injuries are nearly completely healed, I need to concentrate on my mind. The clubhouse ain't exactly peaceful or relaxing, and I need my own space, for Beau and for me. I hope you understand."

Dad's quiet for a moment, taking all I've said in and thinking it through. I'm starting to question what I've said as I really hope he doesn't think I'm being ungrateful.

"I understand, sweetheart. I don't like it. I want you and Beau close. I've missed so much time with you both, but I'm not going to be selfish and put my needs before yours. I just need you both safe. We will talk to Prez and see if he knows of somewhere safe and protected so you can still have your freedom and peace, but are safe too."

Throwing my arms around his waist, I snuggle into his chest. He wraps his big arms around me and kisses the top of my head. I've missed my daddy so much.

"I'll always try to do what is best for you and help you in any way I can. I love you," Dad says softly.

"I love you too, Dad, thank you."

Taking a moment to compose myself and enjoy being with my dad, I pull away.

"Come on. I think Prez is in his office. Let's go see him now," Dad says.

Walking through the clubhouse, we knock on the office door.

"Come in," answers Prez.

Walking in, I let Dad take the lead.

"Got a sec BJ?"

"Sure, you two, what's up?" he says.

Dad explains how my therapy is going and how I need to stand on my own two feet.

His reply irritates me.

"Carrie, have you spoken to Joker about this?"

Looking down, I try to think of the right words to use.

"With all due respect, it's not his decision. I'm not going to stop him from seeing Beau. I would never do that. I need this for my own sanity. Joker and I are not together. I need to provide for Beau and me."

With a nod of his head, he clasps his hands together.

"I understand that Carrie, and that's not why I asked. Joker came to us with an idea. We bought the land to the west of the clubhouse and have been building houses on it. The first house should be ready in the next week or so. That house is yours and Beau's," he says as a matter of fact.

Completely shocked, I start to open my mouth, but then close it again. I don't know what to say. Joker has done this for us. He's ensured I have my own space and freedom, but I'm still safe. Tears fill my eyes.

"I didn't know," I sniffle.

Dad reaches for me and holds me tight.

"That boy loves you and Beau. He's going to want you safe," continues Prez.

Nodding, I take a few minutes to get a hold of my emotions.

"Pip was planning on taking you shopping for furniture in the next few days and to see Nitro about the paint too."

"Thank you, Prez. I need a job now to pay for all the stuff I'm going to need for the house. This means so much to me," I add.

Nodding his head, he gives my dad a look.

"Leave the job with me. I'll see what I can do. The furniture is all paid for. You just need to choose what you like."

Feeling a little shocked, I thank Prez and leave Dad in his office. I need to lie down.

Back in my room, I curl up on the bed and take a few deep breaths. This is a lot to take in. I understand their need to keep Beau and me safe after everything that had happened, but I also need them to talk to me. I'm more than capable of making decisions for myself. So much was out of my control, and so many choices were taken away from me. I need to be in control of my life. I need to explain to Joker how this has made me feel. Feeling a little calmer, I head out to find Joker. I find him in the main room with some of the brothers.

"Joker, do you have a minute, please? I need to talk with you."

He looks up from the plans he is going over with Cass and Nitro.

"Sure, I'll catch up with you guys later," he says.

Getting up, he follows me outside. I need space for this conversation. Sitting at the same picnic table I'd sat at earlier with Dad, I wait for him to sit.

"I spoke with Prez earlier. I know about the house. I want you to know I appreciate you doing this for Beau and me, but this is something you should have spoken to me about. I should have been asked if this was something I wanted or needed. You made all these decisions for me without talking to me first."

He looks taken aback by my comments.

"I did what I thought was right and what you needed. You don't sound grateful," he says, sounding confused.

Yeah, I knew this was not going to go down well.

"I need you to see this from my point of view, Joker. Men have taken my choices and right to choose away from me for so long. I need to reclaim my right to decide. I understand why you did it, and I honestly am grateful. I just need you to understand how you not talking to me makes me feel," I explain.

Taking a deep breath, I hope he's listening and understanding what I'm saying. Running both his hands over his head in frustration, he replies with

"Fuck, Carrie, I didn't mean it like that. I'm only trying to make sure you and Beau are safe. I'm doing what I can. You keep me at arm's length. You won't let me in."

He's getting angry. This is not what I wanted. I knew he wouldn't understand.

"I understand that, but honestly, I'm just trying to reclaim me. You mean a lot to me, Joker. We have our history and Beau together. I'm not the same girl you knew. But I need to be able to stand on my own. Why can't you understand this?"

I'm getting angry now, and from the look on his face, he's getting angrier.

"What, am I not good enough for you anymore? You don't need me? You've got Beau, so who cares about me. Jesus, you're even calling me Joker. I'm not Joker to you, never have been. I'm Jason. Your Jason. I'm supposed to mean something to you. You mean everything to me, Carrie. I never stopped looking for you. I never gave up. Why can't you just let me the fuck in," he exclaims.

By the end of his rant, he's standing shouting at me. His hands are flying around. I can't help my natural reaction, and I flinch.

The horror that crosses his face when he realizes I flinched is heartbreaking. I can't cope with this. I jump up and take off running. I can hear Joker screaming my name, but I keep running. Running through the woods that surround the clubhouse, I keep running until I hit the fence and then run along it. The land the clubhouse is built on is massive, so I have plenty of places to hide until I can get myself together. I feel like I've been running for a long time. I come across what seems to be an old shack of some kind. The door is locked, but one of the windows is open. I pull it open more so I can fit through. I pull myself through the gap, closing the window behind me.

There is a room in the back with an old cot in it. Sitting on the cot, I try to catch my breath. Clearly, I need to start exercising more as I didn't realize how unfit I'd gotten. It's starting to get dark and looking around the room, I find a cupboard that has some blankets in it. I wrap a blanket around me to keep the chill in the air away. I know I'm not going to stay here all night. I just need some space. Between Joker and my dad constantly needing to know where I am and what I'm doing, I'm starting to feel a little suffocated. I need room to think and collect my thoughts.

Hearing someone outside the shack, I keep really still. There are no windows in this room so they can't see in.

"Keep looking as she can't have gone far," says one voice.

"The shack is still locked and the windows are all closed and locked, so we'll keep moving," says another.

I keep still and try to keep my breathing slow. I'm not sure who the voices belong to, but I know Joker and my dad would have all the brothers looking for me. Great, they couldn't even let me have a little peace and space to myself. I know it's because they care and just want me safe, but I've been trapped for so long, I need some freedom.

I've been in the shack a while now, so I decide it's best to head back and face the music. Beau will be worried. Climbing back out of the window, I slowly make my way through the woods. Coming across the clearing, I find a newly built street with the makings of a couple of houses. These must be the houses my dad and Prez were talking about. One house does look finished, and it's beautiful. A wrap-around porch at the front leads me to a large front door. Trying the door, it opens. The entrance is bright and has a warm feel, leading into a living space. A huge fireplace takes up one wall. There's no furniture yet. An arched opening leads off the living space into a huge kitchen dining area. The first things I notice are the granite worktops and a huge oven. Opening another door, I find a larger room with a massive fridge and freezer, plus a laundry room. It's all so beautiful with hardwood floors. Making my way upstairs, I find a huge bathroom and 3 bedrooms. The master has an ensuite bathroom too. It really is perfect. Looking out the window of a bedroom at the rear, I can see an enclosed garden with a barbeque and seating area. Whoever had designed this house put a lot of thought and effort in.

I could see myself being happy here. If only Joker would have talked to me. I don't need someone to care for me. I need someone who will treat me like their equal. Jason is a biker, the alpha male, so I know he's always going to be a caveman. I was afraid of this and knew it would hurt too much when we wouldn't work out. Leaving the beautiful house, I find Pip sitting on the steps outside.

"I knew you would find your way here," she says without turning to me and patting the step next to her. I take a seat beside her, and I wait quietly.

"That boy loves you, but he's an idiot. They all are," she states.

Okay, that is not what I had thought she was going to say.

"They always have your best interests at heart, but rarely do they use their brains. Bloody alpha biker cavemen," she says exasperated. "I've been warning them all to give you the space you need."

This has me smiling.

"Is everyone mad?" I ask.

"Why would they be mad at you? Reck was after killing Joker. Brothers had to hold him back. They're mad at Joker for being an idiot. Kate gave him one hell of an earful, and Beau is refusing to speak to him for upsetting you," explains Pip.

I can just see Kate telling Joker exactly how she feels. I frown when I think of Beau disrespecting his dad like that.

"I'll talk to Beau about his behavior when I get back," I state.

"You'll do no such thing. A boy should be sticking up for his momma."

Giggling a little, she wraps her arm around me and pulls me in for a hug.

"Don't be too hard on them all when we get back," she tells me.

We stay cuddled on the steps for a little longer until the sound of a vehicle pulling up makes us look up. Prez is jumping out of one of the club's SUVs.

"Gave us a bit of a scare there, girly," he says as he reaches us.

"I'm sorry. He was getting so angry and not listening to anything I was saying. I just needed space," I try to explain.

"I understand that. Ready to head back?" he asks.

Nodding, we climb into the SUV and head back to the clubhouse. Walking through the common room, no one says anything. My dad and Joker are nowhere to be seen. I head straight to Beau's room. He's sitting on his bed, playing a handheld game.

"Momma, your back!" He jumps off the bed and gives me a cuddle.

"I'm sorry I scared you, sweetie," I say, kissing his head.

"You didn't scare me. I knew you just needed Momma time. I'm mad at Dad for shouting at you. It was so funny watching Aunt Kate tell Dad off," he tells me with a giggle.

I bet it was.

"Come on, kid, bedtime," I declare.

Getting Beau sorted for bed, and all tucked in, I finally make it back to my room.

Deciding a nice relaxing bath is in order. I light some candles and relax in the bubbles. Soaking my muscles helps me relax and unwind. My mind is still thinking about Joker. We need to be able to co-parent. He has to understand how his actions make me feel. I let my eyes fall closed as I relax further into the hot water.

CHAPTER SIXTEEN

JOKER

"What, am I not good enough for you anymore? You don't need me? You've got Beau, so who cares about me. Jesus, you're even calling me Joker. I'm not Joker to you, never have been. I'm Jason. Your Jason. I'm supposed to mean something to you. You mean everything to me, Carrie. I never stopped looking for you. I never gave up. Why can't you just let me the fuck in?" I exclaim.

By the end of my rant, my arms are flying around, and I'm shouting. She flinches. It stops me dead in my tracks. Holy fuck, she flinched. She thinks I'm going to hit her. Before I can say or do anything, she takes off running.

Screaming her name, she doesn't stop. I start to go after her, but hands grab me and pull me back.

"Get off me. CARRIE!" I'm still shouting for her.

"Leave her be. Give her a little time," Dad tells me.

"The fear on her face, Dad, I would never hurt her," I say as I drop back down onto the bench. My head is in my hands.

I'd never forget the look of fear on her face and the fact I put it there.

"I'm going to fucking kill you," someone shouts, and I'm dragged off the bench by my cut. Brothers come running, but I don't fight back. Reck has every right to kick my ass for scaring her. Reck is pulled off me and I see Beau standing off to the side.

"Son," I call out to him.

He shoots daggers at me and storms into the clubhouse. Great, he's mad at me too.

"You stupid, ape-like son of a bitch," Kate spits at me.

Guess everyone is mad at me.

"You know what she's been through, yet you couldn't simply talk to her and ask her what she wants? No, you just did what you want for her. Then when she tries to explain why that would upset her, you get angry at her. Great work, dipshit! I wouldn't be surprised if you lost her altogether now. She doesn't need taking care of. We all know she can do that herself. She made it back here by herself, didn't she? She needs someone who is her equal. Fuck you, cavemen bikers really are all the same." Kate's rant knocks me on my ass. How did I get this so wrong?

She storms off into the clubhouse. Fuck I hope she's not right. I don't want to lose her. Beau is standing near the door, looking at me with pity. Great, he didn't need to see my verbal ass-kicking by Kate.

"Come on, up ya get," Tank says as he reaches a hand out to help me off the ground.

"Let's take a ride," he adds.

I know he's right and I need to clear my head. I also need to find Carrie.

"Others are looking for her. She can't get out of the compound so give her the space she needs, brother," he says like he's just read my mind or some shit.

Nodding, I head for my bike and take off for a while. Stopping at a little diner on the edge of town, we grab a table in the back.

"Wanna talk about it?" Tank asks as we look over the menu.

"I fucked up. I know I did. I'll never forget the fear in her eyes, brother. She was scared of me. Scared of me, I would never hurt her. She should know this," I say, feeling more confused than I have ever been in my whole life.

"Think of her situation, Joker. How has she been treated, and she's not seen you since she was a teen. I'm sorry to say this, brother, but you're different people now," he explains.

"I'm not different. I'm the same person I've always been," I state.

He gives me a look as if to say, really?

Thinking about it, am I still the same person? Being part of the club and seeing the things I have, has changed me. I'm a little harder now, more jaded with my view on the world we live in. The things that happened to Carrie are also going to change who she is as a person and the way she views things in life.

I'm such a fucking idiot. I just want her safe and happy. I go off without asking her, and then when she tries to explain how she feels, I don't listen. Tank looks at me as if he knows I finally understand.

"I've lost her," I say, defeated.

"I don't think you've lost her, but I do think you've made things harder for yourself, brother."

Trust Tank to give it to me straight. It's why we're so close, always honest with each other.

"You're going to have to work hard and show her that you get it. She'll need space and understanding. Nothing is going to happen overnight, so be prepared to put the work in and wait for her to be ready," he advises.

Yeah, I can see this being a long road.

"I've lost my appetite. Let's head back so I can check she's at least okay."

Nodding in agreement, Tank and I leave the diner and head back to the compound. We've been gone a couple of hours, so I pray to God they found her, and she's okay.

Pulling back into the compound, Prez is outside waiting for us.

"She's in her room, brother. Pip found her at the house you built," he explains.

Letting out a sigh of relief, I head inside and upstairs. Hovering outside her door, I'm not sure whether to knock or give her space. Deciding I need to at least apologize, I knock on the door. Getting no answer, I knock louder. No answer again, so I go to check on Beau. Maybe she's with him.

In Beau's room, he's fast asleep in bed. Wondering if she's okay, I try the adjoining door, finding it open. The room is empty, but steam is showing clearly on the mirror, and the bathroom door is cracked open. Peeking in, I can see she's asleep in the bath. Backing out and pulling the door back, too, I knock on the bathroom door and lightly call her name. I don't want to startle her.

"Carrie, are you in there?" I ask.

I hear splashing through the door.

"Shit. Yeah, I'll be out in a minute. I fell asleep," she calls back to me.

"Okay, I'll wait out here for you," I say, figuring it best to warn her I'll be in the room. Sitting on the bed, I wait for her to come out of the bathroom. It's not long before she joins me.

"I just wanted to talk about earlier," I say.

"I'm sorry I ran. I couldn't take the look of horror on your face," she says with her head down. Placing my fingers under her chin, I gently lift her face to look at me.

"Don't hide from me, Carrie. I'll never hurt you. I promise. I was horrified that my behavior had caused you fear. That had nothing to do with anything you had done. I'm so fucking sorry. I should have listened to you, and I should have asked you what you needed and wanted."

She looks shocked.

"Thank you for understanding." Her voice is so small, but you see her body start to relax after my apology.

"I only had yours and Beau's best interests at heart. I wasn't thinking. I'll try to be better. I can't promise I won't put my foot in it again, but I'll make an effort not to."

That gets a little chuckle out of her and a soft smile.

"Thank you, Jason," she whispers.

My heart beats a little faster when she says my real name. Baby steps, we just need to take things slowly.

"How is everything going with the counseling?" I ask.

"It's going great. Dr. Wood is amazing. She's really patient and is making me see how I can move forward. It's never going to go away. I'll always have the memories, but I'm learning to live with them," she explains.

Nodding, I'm happy she's learning to cope.

"If the scars bother you, see Sketch. He's a brother and also a tattoo artist. He runs Havoc Ink. I'm sure he can come up with a design to turn them into something positive and beautiful," I tell her.

Looking over at her, she has tears running down her face.

"Carrie, I'm sorry. What did I do?" I'm frantic, I've upset her again.

"I'm sorry, you didn't do anything. I just love the idea of making something horrible into something beautiful. I'm not sure I'm ready to be undressed near another man yet, but I'll definitely think about it," she says with a little more hope in her eyes that wasn't there before.

Relief flows through me. Thank God, I haven't upset her again so soon.

"Whenever you're ready, I'll be happy to go with you if that will make you feel more comfortable," I ask.

Seconds after saying that, she moves to hug me. Having her in my arms again is heaven. I know in that minute I'll wait for the rest of my life for her to be ready, and I'll do all in my power to prove to her that I'm the right man for her.

Holding her close for a little longer, I kiss her head and pull away.

"I'll leave you to get sorted after your bath," I say softly.

I get up and head to the door.

"Jason?"

I stop in my tracks and turn to face her.

"Thank you," she says.

Nodding, as I'm not sure I can find words right now, I head for the room I'm staying in. At least this day ended better than it started.

Over the next few days, we work tirelessly on finishing the house, and we go shopping for furniture. Carrie loves the house and that makes me happy. When we were younger, we would dream of what our future would be like, and I remember all the little things Carrie had said she wanted for her dream house. They are all in the house we've built. I'm not sure she remembers mentioning them as she's not said anything, but hopefully, once she and Beau have moved in, she'd start to notice.

Moving in day comes fast, and Beau loves having his own space. His bike that his Gramps and Grandpop got him, which matches mine, sits next to mine in the driveway. He had rode next to me from the clubhouse to the house. When Carrie saw us, she'd laughed and took a few photos. His little electric version is freaking ace, and the guys all gave him a cut too. It says future prospect on it. The kid looks like a mini version of me in his jeans, black boots, t-shirt, and cut, and I couldn't be prouder. He's definitely going to be a handful as he grows up.

I'm sitting on the back deck with a beer, relaxing a little after moving everything in. Carrie has everything in the right rooms, and now it's just a case of putting it all where she wants it. Carrie comes to join me with her own beer.

"That's enough for one day. I'm looking forward to a bath in that amazing bathroom and then a good night's sleep in my new bed," she says as she settles into the chair next to me. She looks happier now she's got her own space.

"I'm glad you like it all," I say as I turn to look at her.

"Don't play coy with me, Jason Davis. Don't for a second think I didn't notice the touches around the house are the same ones we talked about as kids. I can't believe you remembered." Her eyes are getting all misty.

I smile, knowing she had noticed.

"Of course, I remembered. I promised you a dream then, and now I'm making good on that promise," I state.

"Thank you, Jason." She's a little choked up. I'm glad it means so much to her.

With a kiss on my cheek, she whispers, "Goodnight."

Soon I'm alone on the back deck, watching her walk away from me. I can still feel her soft lips on my cheek. Maybe there really is hope for us. Finishing my beer, I lock up and head back to the clubhouse.

Dropping back on my bed, it still smells of her. Closing my eyes, I can feel her hand on my chest as she reached up to kiss my cheek. Undoing my jeans, I grab my hard as steel cock in my hand and start to rub up and down. Remembering how soft her skin felt and how good she felt in my arms. It isn't long before I feel the tell-tale tingle in my balls, and I am shooting my load over my hand and t-shirt.

Feeling a little more relaxed, I strip, dumping clothes in the hamper, and head for the shower. The hot water feels good over my muscles, relaxing me some more. I go to check on Beau after my shower. His bed is empty. Sighing and dropping my head forward, at that moment, I'd forgot he wasn't there. Force of habit, I guess. I miss being so close to the kid. Giving up, I head to bed.

It's been a few months now since Carrie and Beau had moved into the house. Prez got Carrie a job in the club's garage, keeping the boys in check and the office in order. Plus, the garage is always protected, so it's safe for her, with the brothers always coming and going. She seems to love it, and she's really good at it. The office has never been so organized. I'm so proud of the progress she's made, seeing Dr. Wood has done wonders for her. She's more confident every day and is comfortable with the brothers and male customers. Beau is now like a normal kid. He's started school and doing well. Carrie took him to see Dr. Wood also to help him readjust to life.

My phone ringing draws me out of my thoughts.

"Yup," I answer.

"Get to the garage. It's Carrie."

That is all Wrench says before I'm running for my bike and gunning full throttle for the garage. I pull up five minutes later, nearly dropping my bike in my haste to get to Carrie. Running into the garage, Carrie is curled up in Tank's lap, shaking with tears running down her face.

"What the fuck?" I ask

Hearing my voice, Carrie is up and flinging herself into my arms. Wrapping her up as tight as I can, I hold her to me.

"It's okay, babydoll. I've got you."

I try to reassure her, stroking her head.

"Does someone want to tell me what the fuck happened?" I growl.

Tank and Wrench look at each other, and I know this is not going to be good. It's then I spot the blood on the floor and a few drops on Carrie.

My eyes find Tank, and he nods his head.

"Seems one of the customers who came in, Carrie recognized as one of that sick fuck's friends. She knew from his face that he also recognized her. He grabbed her, but she fought him and stabbed him with scissors from the desk. We came running when we heard her shouting. The girl is a badass, waited until we had moved the body and closed the garage before she let go," he explains.

Holy fuck!

Kissing the top of her head, I hold her tighter.

"Fuck, babydoll, you did the right thing. I'm sorry this happened. I promise I'll keep you more protected."

Sniffling, she moves to look at me.

"No, Joker, I can't let this send me backward. I refuse to let this rule my life. The chances of this happening again are slim. But I want to be able to protect myself better. Tank has agreed to show me self-defense, and I was hoping you would agree to give me some refresher training with a gun? It has been years since I have shot properly."

Her strength and courage are inspiring. My girl is strong as fuck.

"Of course, I will, babydoll. Anything you want to feel safer. That said, you're clearly badass with a pair of office scissors," I joke.

This gets a laugh out of her.

"Never going to look at a pair of scissors the same again," Wrench says, shaking his head as he chuckles.

"Come on, I'll take you home," I say.

Nodding to the boys, I know they'd clean the mess up and get rid of the evidence.

Guiding Carrie toward my bike, I find a hoodie in my saddle bag for her to wear.

Climbing on, I hold my hand out for her to get on. Once she's on and snuggled up close to my back with her hands wrapped around me, she whispers in my ear

"Can we go for a ride, please?"

She starts stroking her hand on my stomach to reassure me she's okay. Fuck she feels right on my bike.

"Anything you want, babydoll," I reply.

Starting the bike, I head out of the garage and onto the road. Just driving in any direction, we ride for about an hour. The longer we ride, the more relaxed she becomes. My girl always did love being on a bike. After riding for a little longer, I pull over to a beautiful spot and turn the engine off.

She stays on the bike, with her arms still wrapped around me. I'm not going to complain. I love the feel of her wrapped around me and her warmth at my back. After a little longer, she gets off and stretches.

"Been a while, huh?" I ask.

Getting off the bike, I take her hand in mine. It fits perfectly.

Smiling at me, we take a stroll along the trail. Not talking, just holding hands, and enjoying each other's company. We find a clearing with some benches and take a seat.

"Thank you for coming earlier," Carrie whispers.

"Carrie, I'll always come when you need me," I reassure her.

She rests her head on my shoulder and sighs. I wrap my arms around her and hold her close to me.

"You make me feel safe," she whispers again, and I only just hear it, but boy does it have me smiling at her little admission. I kiss the top of her head.

"You will always be safe with me, babydoll," I confirm.

Deciding to be brave while she's relaxed and being open, I say, "Carrie, my love for you has never faded.

I've been giving you the space and time you need. But I hope you know I would love for us to be a family. I still love you and would love to have a chance. I understand if that is something you can't give me yet or if ever, but I'm willing to wait," I declare.

She's so quiet, but she doesn't pull away from me, which is a good sign.

"Jason, I would like that too. I want to try. I can't promise you anything, but I'm willing to try. We would need to start slow and build it up. I'm sorry I can't give you more than that right now," she admits with a somber expression.

"Babydoll, that means the world to me. I understand you want to take things slow. You set the pace, and I'll follow your lead. Thank you for giving me a chance, giving us a chance," I say, trying hard to keep my excitement at bay.

The look on her face is priceless. Stroking my finger down her cheek, she closes her eyes.

"Kiss me, please," she whispers.

No way can I say no to that. Slowly lowering my head to hers, I gently touch my lips to hers, softly at first, until she whimpers, and then I deepen the kiss, holding her tighter to me. I glide the tip of my tongue across her lips until she opens and lets me in. The kiss deepens until we're battling to pour all our emotions into this one kiss. Slowly pulling away, we're both breathless, and my cock is pushing against my zipper. Fuck, that's the best kiss I have ever had.

CHAPTER SEVENTEEN

CARRIE

My lip still tingles after he had pulled away. Touching my lips, I look up at him. He had a smirk across his face.

"Fuck, babydoll, I've missed you," he says, making me smile.

Kissing me again, I wrap my arms around his neck and back, pulling him closer. I can feel his erection pressing into me, making me pull back. Fuck, this is getting a little too far ahead.

He places his hand under my chin and lifts my head to look at him.

"At your pace, Carrie. You tell me what you're ready for. There's no rush. I'm more than happy kissing and holding you," he reassures.

Giving him a soft smile, I nod my head. Not sure I could form words or form full sentences at the moment. He'd turned me to mush, and I can't think straight.

Taking my hand, he leads me back to his bike. God, I love being on the back of his bike. I'm definitely my father's daughter. It's in my blood. The freedom you feel while riding is just amazing. Getting back on the bike, he goes the long way back to the clubhouse. Guess he loves me being on his bike as much as I do.

Pulling through the gates, I can see my dad, Bull, and Prez outside. Getting off the bike, Jason parks it in line with the others, and we walk to join them. As soon as I'm within reach, Dad pulls me in for a hug.

"You okay, girlie?" he asks.

Holding him back tighter, my dad is my other safe place. A girl should always be able to rely on her daddy.

"Yeah, Dad, I'm good," I reply.

He still holds me a little longer before letting go, when both Bull and Prez surprise me and pull me in for hugs too. These men would die to protect me, and I'll never take that for granted. We're a family, and family protects each other and have each other's backs.

"I'm going to find Beau," I announce.

"He's on the playground, Princess," Prez tells me.

I still get goosebumps when anyone calls me Princess. They're right, I'm the motherfucking Sons of Havoc Princess, and I need to start acting like it. Nodding, I head toward the playground. I find Tank and Kate sitting at one of the tables watching Beau play.

"Hey guys," I say, joining them.

Sitting next to Tank, he wraps an arm around me and draws me into him.

"You okay, Gorgeous?" he asks.

I smile at the nickname he's always called me.

"Yeah, I'm good. How's the kid been?"

"He's way too much like Joker," Kate laughs.

"Yeah, kid's a real chip off the old block. Going to give me a hell of a time when he gets older," I laugh.

"Nah, he'll be good, or one of us will kick his ass," Tank jokes.

"Speaking of ass-kicking, remember when we talked about self-defense. Well, I've been thinking, and I don't want to just do a little self-defense. I want you to train me," I state.

Tank looks at me, a little shocked.

"Oh, I'm up for this too," Kate says.

"Really? Both of you?" questions Tank.

Both of us nod.

"This world ain't safe, and it's not rainbows. I need to know I can get down and dirty when I need to. We all need to be strong and fuck off if you think I'm going to be the weakest link," I say.

I put my hand up before he can say anything.

"I've already talked to Joker, and he's agreed to give me a refresher with a gun. Wolf also said he'd train me with a knife. If you don't want to train me to fight, then I'll speak to Wolf."

He runs his hand over his head and down his face.

"You're serious about this?" he asks.

"Yes, I'm serious. That boy out there means everything to me. I'm his mom. It's my job to protect him and keep him safe. I haven't been able to do that for the first ten years of his life, but I'm sure as hell going to do it from now on," I declare.

Kate and Tank are quiet for a moment.

"I'm in. About time we girls learned to kick ass," adds Kate excitedly.

"Okay, I'll train you both, but the second you're not taking it seriously, I'm done."

We both nod our agreement.

"Right, I need to go shopping as I have no workout-appropriate clothes," I state.

"I'll watch Beau," says Tank.

Nodding and kissing Tank on the cheek, I head for my car with Kate. Girls' shopping trip it is.

It's been a few months now since Tank started training Kate and me. We meet in the club's gym at the compound every morning. True to his word, Tank has not held back. I'm bruised and sore, but fuck, I feel good, and I feel strong. Joker has also been training me with different guns, to clean them, break them down, and also how to shoot them. He bought me a Glock of my own. I love it. All black and looking sexy. He said he'd looked at a pink one, but decided black was the way to go. I agree. Wolf also got me a set of my own knives. I love throwing them. I'm a really good shot now. Angel had offered to teach Kate how to shoot, but Cass went mad, and now he's teaching her. I don't know what the hell is going on with those two, but something is. I'm sure they'll work it out, but it will be a mess if Kate keeps flirting with the brothers and Cass keeps threatening them.

Over the past few months, Joker and I have been dating. We've not had sex yet, but we've kissed a lot. But all the training and my sessions with Dr. Wood have made me feel ready.

I've got a check-up today with Dr. Whitelaw to go over the results. I'm nervous. She was thorough with her tests, and we had to wait a few months for some of the results to make sure nothing developed. I've been to her office for further tests. On the smear test she did first, they found some abnormal cells, so she wanted me to get another to double-check. I'm scared that what they did to me has damaged me. I haven't told anyone. If it's bad news, then I'd tell them, but if it's nothing to worry about, I don't want to panic them for no reason.

Pulling up to her office, I park and head inside. Once I've checked in at reception, I wait. I'm shocked when Joker walks through the door.

"What are you doing here?" I ask.

"I came to support you. I know you were nervous, but I feel like you're not telling me something, so I came anyway," he admits.

Jesus, he always could read me.

"I'm sorry I didn't want to worry you," I apologize.

"We're in this together, Carrie. You don't have to face things on your own," he reassures.

Before we can talk anymore, my name is called. We head to Dr. Whitelaw's office. The nurse hands me a gown and tells me to get comfy on the bed. Going behind the curtain, I remove my clothes and put the gown on. Coming back out, Joker had moved a chair so he can sit at my head. I sit on the bed and wait for Dr. Whitelaw.

"Hello, Carrie. Oh, hello, Jason," Dr. Helen says, surprised.

Joker shakes her hand. "Hey, Dr. Whitelaw," he greets.

"Please call me Helen. Right so how are you feeling, Carrie?" she asks.

"I'm nervous. I feel okay, though," I admit.

Nodding, she makes some notes on the computer on her desk.

"That's good. There is nothing to be nervous about. Okay, so if you'll just lie back and place your feet in the stirrups. Relax, and we'll start the exam," she states.

Lying back and getting as comfy as I can, Joker grabs my hand. I'm now really grateful he's here. Dr. Whitelaw does the examination. It's uncomfortable, but not painful.

"Thank you, Carrie, you can sit up now," Dr. Helen declares.

Sitting up, Joker still doesn't release my hand.

"Everything is looking perfect. You've healed great, and there is no lasting scarring. I know we spoke last time about the smear test showing abnormal cells and what that could mean," she says.

Nodding my head, I don't speak.

"What could abnormal cells mean?" Joker asks.

"Abnormal cells can mean a number of things, a change in hormone levels, infection, but they can also be an indicator of cancer," she explains.

Joker looks at me and squeezes my hand tighter.

"However, the second smear test came back negative. We would like to monitor you more closely, so I'd like to see you again in six months for another smear test. If all is okay, you can go back to your regular timescale. All your other blood work and tests came back negative also," she declares.

I let out a breath I didn't realize I was holding, and tears start to run down my face. Joker gets up and pulls me into a hug.

"I'll give you two a moment. You can get dressed now, and I'll see you in 6 months," she adds.

"Thank you, Helen," I manage to get out between sobs.

Joker holds me tighter while Helen leaves us alone.

"Carrie, Babydoll, why didn't you tell me?" asks Joker.

"I was too scared," I admit.

He holds me tighter for a little longer until I manage to stop crying. Once I manage to get myself together,

I get dressed. On the way out we make another appointment for six months' time. Outside, Joker pushes me up against the truck and kisses me like it's our last.

"Fuck when she said cancer, my heart dropped. Don't ever do that to me again, Carrie. I just got you back. I can't lose you," he blurts out.

Before I can answer, he's kissing me again. God, this man turns me to mush. Joker finally releases me from his hold, and I move to open the door to my truck.

"I'll meet you back at the house. Beau is staying with Kate tonight," Joker tells me.

Nodding, I get in the truck and drive to my house in a daze. Pulling into the drive, Joker is already waiting there and has my door open before I've managed to grab my bag. Lifting me from the truck, he carries me into the house and upstairs, placing me on the bed. He goes into the bathroom, and I hear the water running. Then he's back in the bedroom.

"Go relax in the bath, Babydoll. I'll cook dinner," he orders.

Kissing my head, he's gone.

Walking into the bathroom, I notice he had lit some candles and put bubbles in the bath.

Removing my clothes, I place them in the hamper, and I step into the bath. The heat and bubbles relax me. I'm not sure how long I have been lying there, but delicious smells reach me from the kitchen, making me realize how hungry I am. Getting out of the bath, I dry off and put my robe on. Deciding not to bother with underwear, I pad bare footed downstairs, following the smell. The sight that greets me is amazing. The table is all set with candles, my favorite pasta dish with garlic bread, and two beers are waiting.

"How was your bath?" Joker asks.

Turning to the voice, I see Joker in the kitchen, shirtless and with jeans hanging off his hips. My mouth is suddenly dry. Chuckling, he comes over to me and guides me to a chair at the table.

"Why didn't you tell me about the tap? I'm soaked. I'll sort it tomorrow for you," he states.

Rolling my eyes, I giggle. The tap in the kitchen had been playing up and keeps squirting water everywhere.

"I meant to tell you," I admit.

Now it's his turn to roll his eyes.

"You've been meaning to tell me a lot of things, Babydoll. No more meaning to tell me, please. Honesty from now on?" he asks.

I know he's not talking about the tap anymore. Nodding, I tuck into my pasta. I can't help but make a moaning sound. The clanking of metal makes me jump. I didn't realize my eyes had closed.

Joker is staring at me with heat and lust in his eyes. Dropping my head down to look at my plate, I murmur an apology with a slight giggle.

We chat through our meal, mainly about Beau. Joker clears the table. As he gets up, I can see his erection pressing into the front of his jeans. I really have been torturing him without meaning to. Dr. Wood had told me I need to be braver and grab what I want in life. Deciding she's right, I'm going to grab what I want. While his back is to me, I untie my robe and grip the edges.

"Joker," I call.

"Yeah," he replies.

As he turns around to look at me, I slowly move the robe over my shoulders and down my arms, revealing my naked body. I watch his eyes go big as they slowly follow the path of the robe.

"Carrie," he says, his voice all husky.

"I want this. I want you," I declare.

Dropping the robe, so it pools at my feet, I decide to be a little braver to force his hand. I run my fingers over the top of my breasts and circle my nipples. My nipples are now little peaks. I let my head fall back a little as my hands glide lower. Before they even reach my stomach, his hands are on me, lifting me onto the table. Pulling a chair between my legs, he sits down.

"If at any point it gets too much, tell me, and we stop," he orders.

"I promise," my voice husky too.

His hands are running up and down the tops of my thighs as he takes my peaked nipple into his mouth. I gasp as my head falls back. His mouth on my breast feels amazing. He moves from one to the other as his hands get closer to my center.

"Lie back for me, Babydoll. It's time for my dessert," he says seductively.

The lust and love in his eyes have me trusting him and lying down.

The second my back hits the table, his tongue glides over my lips, causing my hips to lift off the table. He puts an arm over my stomach to hold me still as he continues to lick and suck. My whole body is shaking, and I can feel my release building higher. I feel his fingers enter me, and he rubs them along the spot, and I can't stop the scream that rips from me as my release explodes like thousands of fireworks going off all over my body. He continues to gently lick me and kiss me until I come down from my high. My whole body is still shaking. He picks me up and carries me to the bedroom. Laying me on the bed, he strips out of his jeans. Jesus, this man is a work of art. Joining me on the bed, he places a few condoms on the bedside table, and then he kisses my shoulder. Moving onto my side so I can face him, I kiss his lips. I can still taste myself on him. Moaning, I run my hands down his chest and wrap my fingers around his cock. I slowly move my hands up and down. The hiss from him makes me jump and let go.

"Oh God, I'm sorry," I say, horrified.

"Hey, Babydoll, what's wrong?" he asks.

"I'm sorry I hurt you," I tell him, completely mortified this happened.

A little chuckle leaves him, causing me to look at him confused.

"Fuck, Babydoll, you're so fucking cute. You didn't hurt me. I was enjoying it. Keep touching me," he tells me.

Feeling a little better now I know he liked it, I continue to explore his rock-hard cock, cupping his balls with my other hand. He puts his hands behind his head and watches me.

"Fuck, Carrie, I need inside you. I can't take much more of you touching me like this," he admits.

Smiling, I nod. He reaches for the condoms and puts one on.

"Lie back, baby," he says.

I do as he says, and he settles between my legs, with his weight on his hands on either side of my head.

"Is this okay?" he asks, waiting for my permission.

Nodding, I lick my lips. He grabs hold of his cock and lines it up.

"Just relax. I won't hurt you," he declares.

Wrapping my arms around him, I kiss him as he slowly pushes inside of me. I feel so full. He stops and gives me time to get used to him.

Wrapping my legs around him, I beg, "Please move. I won't break and you won't hurt me. Please, Jason."

Saying his real name seems to be the trigger as he pulls out and thrusts back inside me. The pleasure rippling through me is amazing.

"Fuck, you're gripping me so tight. This isn't going to last long. I can't. You're driving me insane," he pants.

His rhythm is erratic as he gets closer to his release, his hands slide between us. The second he touches my clit, I'm gone, screaming his name with him following behind me seconds later. He falls next to me, wrapping his arms around me, pulling my body into his. We lie in each other's arms, just holding each other until we come down and catch our breath.

He kisses my head as he gets off the bed and goes to the bathroom. He comes back a few minutes later with a washcloth and cleans me up. Okay, I know that should be sweet, but it's also a little embarrassing, but I don't say anything. He has the biggest smile on his face, and I don't want to ruin the moment.

He gets back into bed and pulls me into him.

"Thank you for trusting me. I love you, Carrie," he declares.

Smiling up at him, I kiss the end of his nose.

"That was amazing. I love you too, Jason," I admit.

We lay there quietly, my brain working a mile a minute, and before I can stop myself, I blurt out, "Move in."

He pulls away so he can look at me.

"What?" he asks, complete shock on his face.

"Move in. I want us to be a family," I tell him.

Rolling over, he covers my face in kisses.

"You've made me the happiest man in the world twice tonight, Babydoll."

I laugh as he continues to cover my face in kisses.

EPILOGUE

CARRIE

The last few months have been incredible. Joker had moved in with Beau and me. We're a real family like we'd always dreamed of. Beau is going from strength to strength, especially now with his dad living with us.

Joker had mentioned making me his ol' lady a few times, but I've told him I'm not ready for that yet. Baby steps. I understand how important and what it means to him to have me wearing his property patch, but after being *'owned'* for so long by someone else, I'm just not ready to be branded as someone's property. Not even Jason's. We're living together; we have a child together and are building a life with our extended club family together. I'm not going anywhere soon.

Tonight, we're having a huge family barbecue to welcome my little brother as a new patched-in member. Johnny has worked so hard, and I couldn't be prouder of him for earning his patch. Dad has been walking around like he's on cloud nine recently. I know this has something to do with Agnes. I'm happy for them as they both deserve some happiness.

Leaving the clubhouse kitchen, I help the other ol' ladies take the food outside to the long tables that have been set up near the grills. Wolf and Prez are in charge of the barbecue. Beau is playing on the playground with a few of the other club kids. Tank and Joker are drinking beer nearby, watching them. Heading over to them, I slip under Joker's arm. He places a kiss on my head.

"Having fun?" I ask.

"Yeah, Tank was just telling me about this girl he met at the range. Gave him a run for his money," laughs Joker.

Looking over at Tank, he just shrugs his shoulders like it's no big deal.

"She better than me?" I tease.

I've come a long way with my training, and I'm now a better shot than some of the brothers.

"Yeah, gorgeous, she's better than even Gunny," he admits.

My eyes widen at that. Gunny got his name for being a gunnery sergeant. The man could shoot any target and hit dead center. She must be pretty amazing to beat him. Watching Tank, he gets this look in his eye. Yeah, I bet this girl is hot. Trouble always seems to follow hot girls around here.

JOKER

I watch Carrie tease Tank about this girl from the range. Even she can see the look in his eyes. I can see trouble in his future. All women are trouble, but they are worth the pain.

I watch Carrie as she walks around the yard, chatting with everyone and making sure the single brothers have food. I can't drag my eyes from her curves. Fuck, my girl has curves in all the right places, and she drives me wild with how innocent yet trusting she is.

The more we're together, the braver she's becoming with stuff she'd let me do in the bedroom. I never want to do anything that would remind her of what happened. But on the advice of Dr. Wood, we have slowly been trying new things and replacing the bad memories with good. Carrie owns my soul, and I would do anything for her and Beau.

She turns to look at me and winks while running her hand suggestively down her hip. Yeah, my vixen is feeling frisky tonight. I start over to her, throwing my beer in an empty barrel. Reaching her, I press my shoulder into her stomach and pick her up over my shoulder. Striding for the clubhouse, I call to Tank.

"Watch Beau."

We carry on inside to catcalls and whistles.

Fuck I love my life.

THE END

ACKNOWLEDGMENTS

I can't believe I finally finished Joker and Carrie's story. It's been a true labor of love for me as these characters are very close to my heart. I really hope you enjoyed their journey. This is not the end for them or the men of the Sons of Havoc. Next up is Tank. His story is one I cannot wait to bring to life.
There are some people I really wanted to thank.
My wonderful family who has been amazingly supportive. My poor husband, who I think forgot at times he had a wife as I would come home from work, plus weekends, and disappear to write. Thank you for listening to me bounce ideas and also bringing me cups of tea to keep me going.
My book babes, Helen, Kate, and Tracy. Thank you for keeping me going, encouraging me that yes, I can do this and for helping me work out how scenes would go and just keeping me sane. You rock!
My wonderful friends, Charlene, Kelly, Vikki, and Charlotte. Thank you for your support. You have

honestly been amazing when the book is all I could think and talk about.

To the amazing authors who have inspired me, given me advice and guidance when I've been so overwhelmed with it all. Victoria Johns, Victoria L. James, Ellie R. Hunter, Elizabeth Knox, Amy Davies, Ruby Carter and plus every MC writer whose books I have read and loved.

Finally, to you, the readers. Thank you for taking a chance and reading my baby. I hope you loved it as much as me. I promise Tank is on his way and many more of the sons who find their badass other half. Sometimes we don't need saving. We can save ourselves!

Sons Of Havoc
Texas Chapter Series
Joker
Havoc Novella
Tank
Havoc Christmas
Wire – Coming soon

Sons of Havoc
Phoenix Chapter
Bishop – coming soon

ABOUT THE AUTHOR

USA Today Best Selling Author Claire is a Yorkshire lass born and bred. She lives there with her husband, 2 fur babies, and a large crazy extended family.
Claire is also a huge country music fan and has a bit of an eclectic taste.
Claire has been involved with the indie community for many years now, attending signings but also as a PA for authors.
Those authors encouraged Claire to put her ideas and life experiences on paper.
Believing reading is an escape from the pressures of real life, Claire is an avid reader and loves the joy it brings to people!

Facebook

Facebook Group

Instagram

Goodreads

Printed in Great Britain
by Amazon